The King Who Turned into a Serpent
and Other Thrilling Tales of Royalty from Indian Mythology

The King Who Turned into a Serpent

and Other Thrilling Tales of Royalty from Indian Mythology

SUDHA MADHAVAN

illustrated by Priyanka Pachpande

hachette INDIA

First published in 2022 by Hachette India
(Registered name: Hachette Book Publishing India Pvt. Ltd)
An Hachette UK company
www.hachetteindia.com

1

ISBN 978-93-91028-23-7

Hachette Book Publishing India Pvt. Ltd
4th & 5th Floors, Corporate Centre
Plot No. 94, Sector 44, Gurugram – 122003, India

Typeset by Manmohan Kumar, Delhi

Printed and bound in India
by Manipal Technologies Limited, Manipal

MIX
Paper from responsible sources
FSC™ C043100

To my father,
the original storyteller…
…and to little Rishi

CONTENTS

FROM ME TO YOU

The picture is alive in my mind, when rainy nights were dotted invariably with stories. The cosy shelter of the huge verandah as the rains came pouring down… where as a child I sat at my father's feet and listened, fascinated, to stories, often several times over!

The spray of the raindrops, and then the rustle of the leaves, and the twinkling of the stars, when the showers stopped. The clear dark blue of the sky, the enchanting moon and the shimmer of the Milky Way! There was a magic in those nights, which has not faded with time, and the memories linger on. It is like the comforting touch of a fond hand…

The pleasure of hearing a well-told story can be equalled only by the pleasure of telling a good one. In days of yore, in the absence of the television, the computer, video games and suchlike, storytelling was an integral part of childhood. A day was not quite complete without a juicy story at the end of it!

In our country, as in many others, these stories were based on mythological figures, legendary heroes and larger-than-life characters who performed astounding feats of excellence or unimaginable acts of foolishness.

The stories wove a brilliant and kaleidoscopic canvas to leave children wonderstruck with their colour and imagery. They teased the listener's imagination to new heights, creating a space where everything, no matter how impossible, was made real and possible. They left unspoken role models to follow, subtle lessons to imbibe, hilarious recipes for enjoyment and wonder!

However, nothing seemed out of reach in them...

By and large, these were not read out, but pulled out of a treasure trove of tales, much like the magician's rabbit emerging out of the hat! In large families teeming with elders, there was no dearth of stories and tales to tell. Anyone from grandparents to uncles and aunts turned official storyteller.

Of course, there were the favourites who could add a lot of spice and tell one with a flourish.

Often, stories were told to keep naughty children away from their pranks, the talkative ones quiet, and to put the troublesome ones to sleep!

Many carried a relevant, sneaky moral to set an errant child right as well.

All in all, these stories invariably gave a message of good winning over evil, of patience rewarded, and of courage celebrated.

Consequently, they imparted a sense of well-being and hope, arguing (through examples) in favour of what was right. They made exalted values believable and practicable.

Much depends, therefore, on how well a story is told. And how responsibly…

There are so many wonderful, thrilling stories of kings and queens and princes and princesses that even as I recalled and wrote them down for this book, I got the goosebumps!

Telling these stories is as thrilling as hearing them, and I feel fortunate to relate these stories to you and share the joy with you all!

Sudha Madhavan
Bengaluru, 2022

SHISHUPALA, THE KING WHO WAS BORN WITH FOUR ARMS AND A THIRD EYE!

You may have read about the two doorkeepers or *dwarapalakas* of Lord Vishnu – Jaya and Vijaya – who acted a bit too smart with the four sages, the Sanath Kumaras. The duo was cursed to be born on earth as punishment!

Lord Vishnu came to their help by giving them a choice between a hundred good births, or three mighty evil ones on earth! They quickly chose the latter!

Jaya and Vijaya were born as the brothers Hiranyaksha and Hiranyakashipu in the Satya Yuga, as brothers Ravana and Kumbhakarna in the Treta Yuga, and as Shishupala, cousin to Lord Krishna himself, and his cousin Dantavakra in the Dwapara Yuga.

Lord Krishna, as we know, was actually an avatar of Vishnu.

He performed quite a few miracles. He was great friends with the Pandavas, to whom he was related.

He imparted the wonderful 'Bhagavad Gita'. He literally had a finger in every pie, so to say!

A very interesting and charming character!

Among all these things and more, he also took care of his promise to Jaya and Vijaya.

Meanwhile, the hero of our story here is Shishupala, who became the ruler of a small kingdom called Chedi, close to Dwarka, where Lord Krishna ruled.

We must first see, though, how he was a cousin to Krishna.

Hmm… Krishna's father was Vasudeva and his mother was Devaki.

And Shishupala was born to Shrutakirti, Vasudeva's sister and Krishna's aunt. And that makes him cousin to Krishna, of course! Kunti, the mother of the Pandava princes, was the other sister of Vasudeva. And that made Krishna a cousin to the Pandavas as well. With whom, of course, he got along quite famously.

Now we go back to the beginning and the strangest part of the story of Shishupala.

When Shishupala was born, his parents were not happy at all. In fact, they were rather shocked and very sad too.

Now why was that? All parents rejoice at the birth of a new baby in the family, don't they?

But here they had a reason to not feel that way.

Because the baby was born with four arms and a third eye!

They were very worried and spent sleepless nights.

At last, they decided to give the baby away.

However, just as they were about to cast the baby away, they heard a voice from the skies, an *ashariri*!

It said:

'Do not cast the child away. His time is yet to come. He shall die at the hands of the person in whose arms his third eye and extra arms disappear.'

Baby Shishupala's parents were stunned! They stood rooted to the spot, staring up at the sky.

The mother was really worried for her baby now. She was anxious to find out who the enemy to her baby's life was.

But how could she do that?

The only way was to hand her baby to every visitor who came and see whether the extra arms and the third eye disappeared...

And several such people came visiting. Many of them were very inquisitive indeed. Word had spread that at Shrutakirti's house was born a surprising child and they were curious to see this rather strange baby.

'Do you know what I heard?' they whispered to one another in shocked tones.

'Yes, yes, I heard it too! Poor Shruti...' they nodded, feeling sorry for the poor woman. 'Whatever will she do?'

The visitors of course did not know about the *ashariri* that baby Shishupala's parents had heard.

And to every visitor to their house, Shrutakirti handed her baby to hold in their arms for a while. She would watch anxiously while they did so to see whether the extra arms and third eye disappeared or not.

Many such visitors came and went. Baby Shishupala was put into each one's arms, but the third eye and the extra arms remained.

Each time, Shishupala's parents heaved a sigh of relief.

And then one day, their nephew, Krishna, visited them. As was her habit now, his aunt Shrutakirti handed baby Shishupala to him to hold.

And to her shock and dismay the extra arms and third eye disappeared!

'Krishna! You...it is you!' cried his aunt, Shrutakirti. 'How can you do this, Krishna? To your own little cousin!'

'What? What have I done?' exclaimed Krishna, pretending not to know.

'Do you know what the *ashariri* from the skies said? In whosoever's hands baby Shishupala's eye and extra arms disappear, will be his killer. And look, the third eye is no longer there...and the extra arms have gone! Krishna, that means you are Shishupala's enemy. At your hands will he die!'

'Well, Aunt Shruti, I really don't want to be the one to kill Shishupala...' said Krishna sadly. 'And I do feel sorry if it has to happen at my hands! But if it is destined to happen, it will. No one can change that. Not even I!'

'Promise me, Krishna, that no matter what, you will not raise your hand against him,' cried his aunt. 'Promise me now.'

'I promise you, dear aunt, that even if he picks up a fight with me, I shall never retaliate. But...'

'But what, Krishna?' cried his worried aunt.

'But there will be a limit,' Krishna said. 'If he abuses me more than a hundred times, I shall *have* to punish him!'

He was Lord Vishnu, so he knew all about the past, the present and the future, but could he possibly tell anyone about what was going to happen in the future?

No, of course, not. That he kept a secret.

Now getting on with the story...

Young Shishupala grew up, well-trained in the art of war and the use of all weapons, as any prince would be. His best friend was Rukmi, the prince of the kingdom of Vidarbha. He was also friends with Duryodhana, the Kaurava prince and a cousin of the Pandavas.

Despite being a very brave and talented warrior, Shishupala was not blessed with goodness of nature. He was arrogant and ill-mannered. He took a great dislike to his cousin Krishna, the ruler of Dwarka, and picked a fight with him at every possible opportunity.

There was a reason for that too.

When Shishupala was old enough to be married, he chose to marry the lovely, young princess, Rukmini of Vidarbha. She was the younger sister of Rukmi, Shishupala's close friend.

But Rukmini was determined to marry Krishna and no one else!

It so happened that princess Rukmini's father, the king, too wanted her to marry the charming and powerful king of Dwarka, Krishna. However, her brother, Rukmi, would rather that she married his friend, Shishupala.

Rukmini wrote a letter to Krishna, requesting him to rescue her.

Krishna did not waste a moment! He defeated Rukmini's brother Rukmi in a hard-won battle and took away the beautiful Rukmini to be his wife.

Well! We now know at least one of the reasons for Shishupala's deep dislike of Krishna.

Time went by.

Shishupala made it a habit of troubling Krishna whenever he got a chance.

He set fire to Dwarka, when Krishna was away on a battle. He picked a fight with Krishna's friend, King Bhoja, when he was away on a hunt! He even stole Krishna's father Vasudeva's horse just before he was to perform the Ashwamedha Yagna!

For none of these did Krishna do anything to punish Shishupala! He remembered his promise to his aunt Shrutakirti that he would ignore any trouble that his cousin caused. But, with each mischief, Shishupala grew more arrogant. He taunted Krishna, calling him a coward. That he did nothing to answer back because he, Krishna, was afraid of Shishupala's might!

'You are worthless, Krishna,' crowed Shishupala. 'You could not stand up to me, if you tried. No wonder you don't fight back. Ha, ha!'

Krishna kept quiet. He knew how to keep his cool. As Lord Vishnu's avatar, he knew Shishupala's time for punishment had not yet come. Until such time, he would not break the rules.

Several months passed.

King Yudhishthira, the eldest of the Pandava princes and the king of Indraprastha, wanted to be known as an emperor of the world as he was a just and powerful king and well loved by his subjects. He also wanted warring kings to be brought together in friendship.

All this could only be done by performing the Rajasuya Yagna.

The preparations began on a very large scale. All the kings of the various kingdoms were invited to take part in the yagna. They were glad to attend. And, of course, Shishupala, the king of Chedi, was also invited. And Krishna, a close friend and a cousin to Yudhishthira, came as well.

There was much laughter and backslapping among the various kings. Everyone was happy to catch up with each other. The learned rishis shared their knowledge, life experiences and *tapasya*.

Everyone felt honoured to be invited by the generous King Yudhishthira. The king took care to see that all his royal and learned guests were made to feel comfortable and at home!

The guests sat down in the assembly before the yagna began. As was the custom, King Yudhishthira got up to greet his guests.

'My learned gurus, fellow kings and friends,' he said, 'I am honoured by your presence. I am grateful that you could find time to attend my Rajasuya Yagna in spite of your many duties. I welcome you with all my heart. I hope you find everything to your satisfaction. Thank you.'

Then all those present in the assembly were introduced by their name and the kingdom they ruled. And of course, there was one very important formality to be carried out. And what was that?

It was to honour the most respected guest in the gathering and to let everyone know why he was valued above all. Of course, the king took great care to choose the right person for that!

After much thought, Yudhishthira spoke:

'My dear gentlemen! I am sure you will agree with me that Krishna is the one most deserving of the honour!

'He is the Lord himself, the ruler of the three worlds, and knows the past, the present and the future! He is kind-hearted and generous! He is fair and just! He is well-learned in the art of war and the use of weapons, yet he will never use his skill unless it is completely necessary. I am certain that we are all of one mind in this decision.'

There was loud cheer. There were cries of 'Hear! Hear!' Everyone stood up and applauded the choice.

Except one person, of course.

Can you guess who that was?

I am sure you know.

It was Shishupala, the king of Chedi, the cousin and sworn enemy of Krishna.

He neither applauded nor cheered.

He was trembling with anger! His face turned a not very pretty shade of purple! He waited impatiently for everyone else to sit down and the cheering to end.

Then he got up. He raised his voice so that he was heard well by all present.

'My friends!' roared Shishupala in anger, 'I am surprised that you support Yudhishthira's decision! Honour Krishna? My foot! Only he who is deserving of honour, should be honoured! In what way, tell me, is Krishna deserving?

'Is he of royal blood?

'Is he the oldest and the most respected?

'No! I say, No! He is not!

'He is a mere cowherd! He knows nothing more than grazing and milking cows!

'Ha, ha! Should such a person be honoured in this royal assembly?

'Is there no one else more fitting for the honour?

'Of course, there are. And many,' roared Shishupala furiously. 'Yudhishthira is being partial and honouring his friend. Shame on him, I say. My friends, I feel we should oppose this.'

He shook his fist at Krishna.

Everyone sat stunned.

Shishupala went on hurling abuses at Krishna. He just could not stop himself, so angry was he.

Everyone around was shocked. The Pandava brothers tried to calm Shishupala down.

'Sit down, Shishupala, will you?' urged Bheema, who was Shishupala's friend. 'Have the sense to think before you speak!'

'You keep quiet, Bheema – I know what I am about,' shouted Shishupala. 'Don't suck up to your cousin and your brothers if you are a friend of mine!'

Bheema did not know what to do! All the Pandava brothers tried to make peace, fearing the worst. But would Shishupala listen? Not at all! He seemed to be bent on inviting trouble.

Only Krishna was quiet, watching with a half-smile on his face...

He was sad for Shishupala. But, as Lord Vishnu, he also knew that Shishupala was fast keeping the promise that the *ashariri* had made.

Shishupala continued to rain abuses on Krishna. He was unstoppable.

Soon, he reached his limit: the dangerous figure of a hundred abuses!

Krishna stood up and faced the assembly. Everyone turned quiet. There was pin-drop silence!

'My exalted friends,' he said, 'I have not taken any offence until now to all the misdeeds of my cousin, Shishupala, here. He has not missed a single opportunity to trouble me. From the time he set fire to my kingdom of Dwarka, to the time he made away with the sacred horse meant for the Ashwamedha Yagna to be performed by my father, Vasudeva!

'From the time he attacked King Bhoja's kingdom to the many such actions that have caused me endless headaches, I was determined to not raise a finger against him. Now my patience has worn thin. My cousin doesn't seem to realize that keeping quiet is not a sign of weakness, but of strength.

'Today, right here and now, he has crossed his limit of a hundred abuses. He has sorely tested my patience! I had promised his mother, my aunt Shruti, that I shall not let myself be drawn into a fight with him unless he forces me. Now that time has come!

It is his destiny that he should die at my hands. My friends, I am helpless!'

And with that, Lord Krishna let go of his Sudarshana Chakra. The deadly disc flashed across the grand royal chamber. Shishupala's head fell to the ground, and from his body rose an aura that merged with Krishna, who was Vishnu incarnate.

And that was the end of Shishupala. And, with that, Jaya completed his three evil births on earth.

The three births that were a shortcut for him to reach his master's side again.

Back to beautiful Vaikuntha.

Back to his Lord Vishnu.

Shishupala, in his anger, attacked Dwarka several times. In each of these attacks, it was Krishna who won, with the help of Balarama, his brother. But each time he won, he let Shishupala get away alive because Shishupala gathered the worst of allies each time and Krishna was keen to finish them off. Krishna made sure to fight every time for good to win over evil.

JARASANDHA, THE KING WHO WAS BORN IN TWO HALVES

This is indeed one of the most unusual stories that I heard as a child, and still feel thrilled to listen to and to tell it to you all. So here goes…

Once long, long ago, lived a powerful ruler of Magadha, called Brihadratha. He ruled over a large and flourishing kingdom, and married the two princesses of Kashi.

Unfortunately for him, he begot no child and heir.

One day, to his court came sage Chandra Kaushika to whom he lamented about not having an heir.

The kindly sage gave him a fruit, saying, 'O king, please give this blessed fruit to your queen and she will bear you a child.' And he left.

Chandra Kaushika was not aware, of course, that the king had two queens…

Now, the king loved both his queens equally and therefore he gave one half of the fruit to each.

And lo and behold! To them were born in the course of time, a child each. But the joy turned to shock and sorrow…

And why was that, you ask.

Well, *that was because the child was born in two halves, one half to each queen.*

Because they'd each eaten half the fruit.

Would such a child live? Of course not.

So, the king, not knowing what to do, decided to leave the two halves of the child under a tree in the neighbouring forest.

And now we come to the interesting part of the story and the arrival of the future powerful king, Jarasandha!

In that very same forest lived a *rakshasi* (demoness) called Jara. As she was roaming through the forest, she saw, under a tree, a surprising sight…

She stood amazed at the two halves of an infant lying lifeless.

She picked them up in her giant hands.

As she put them together, a most astonishing thing happened!

The two halves joined and …

The baby came alive!

He started crying.

Although she was a demoness who often ate human flesh, she didn't have the heart to kill the baby. She took him to King Brihadratha and told him about the astonishing incident, not knowing that this was his own child whom he had abandoned.

The king was overjoyed to get his child back… whole. He now had an heir to the throne of Magadha.

'Wonder of wonders, I cannot believe,
This miracle child has come alive!
I have now my heart's desire –
An heir to the Magadha empire!'

There was great rejoicing and celebrations across the kingdom. The infant prince was named 'Jarasandha', meaning 'one who was joined together by Jara', the benevolent demoness.

Time passed by.

Chandra Kaushika visited the court once again and gave the king glad tidings: 'Jarasandha will grow up to be a powerful and illustrious ruler of Magadha, and he will be a great devotee of Lord Shiva!'

Well…so the young prince grew up to be a strong and remarkable young man and, in time, became the ruler of Magadha. His kingdom spread far and wide. He was now the emperor of Magadha.

Now we will see how he came to be at loggerheads with Krishna, who was the ruler of the neighbouring kingdom of Mathura.

Years passed and history repeated itself. King Jarasandha did not have an heir to the throne. Hoping for one, he got his two daughters married to Kansa, the then ruler of Mathura, who was uncle to Krishna.

Now, you must know that Krishna and his uncle, Kansa, did not really get along well.

That story went back a long way to their past when Kansa was bent upon killing his nephew Krishna, since he had been warned by an *ashariri*, a celestial voice, that Krishna would be his nemesis.

Along the way, things came to a head between Krishna and Kansa, and Krishna killed Kansa, and became the king of Mathura himself.

Jarasandha's two daughters were widowed. He had no hope for an heir now.

Well. Naturally then, baying for Krishna's blood and boiling for revenge, Jarasandha attacked Mathura.

Now how many times do you think he attacked Mathura?

Once? Twice?

NO!

He attacked Mathura no less than seventeen times.

All of the seventeen times, Krishna, with the help of his brother Balarama, defeated him.

However, the eighteenth time when Jarasandha attacked Mathura, Krishna decided he'd had enough.

He went away to his newly built island capital of Dwarka. It was a fortress city with a strong military and Yadava guards.

None could hope to get in.

However, the story did not end there…

Jarasandha held more than eighty kings captive. He had defeated them and annexed their kingdoms, and they were definitely far from happy.

He meant to do away with them. However, Krishna wanted their release and also an excuse to finish off Jarasandha who was intoxicated with his own power.

As luck would have it, Krishna got the chance to do that as well.

It was when, advised by Krishna, Yudhishthira announced his Rajasuya Yagna to declare his supremacy over all other kings and establish himself as 'emperor of the world'.

And, naturally, he wanted to invite all other kings for this. Therefore, he along with his cousin, Krishna, sought to release the imprisoned kings. This, of course, was impossible with Jarasandha holding them. The only solution was to get rid of Jarasandha.

Hmm…but what was a fair way to do this?

Krishna had to have a hand in it. He was a master strategist, you see!

And Jarasandha was no mean opponent. He was a very powerful emperor and an accomplished wrestler as well. To take an army out to defeat him in battle would definitely not be a great idea.

It was next to impossible to beat him, yet defeat him they must. But how?

Well…a knotty problem indeed.

Upon much reflection, Krishna decided to take Arjuna and Bheema with him to Magadha, all three dressed as mendicant Brahmins. Thinking them to be innocent, Jarasandha allowed them into his presence. No sooner had they entered the court than they shed their disguises and revealed themselves!

'Well, well, who do we have here?' drawled Jarasandha, sitting up. Here was his enemy and at his mercy!

'O king, we are here to invite you to a duel,' spoke Krishna, wasting no time. 'You may choose any one of us as the opponent.'

Jarasandha thought a while. No king could possibly refuse a challenge! Besides, Jarasandha knew no opponent who could defeat him…well, maybe not Krishna or Arjuna. But Bheema?

'I've heard he is a great wrestler…' mused Jarasandha. 'It would be my pleasure to see Bheema bite the dust!' he said, with a smile.

'So be it!' said Krishna. He, of course, had other plans. But he kept those to himself.

And, therefore, it came about that Jarasandha and Bheema locked arms in a wrestling match.

And what a match it was!

Not a moment passed where either of them was not on top of the game…

A hold for a hold. A grapple for a grapple. A throw for a throw.

The match went on for fourteen days. There was no end in sight… Both were equally ferocious, tricky and immeasurably strong.

The match went on and on. A…n…d on!

Every time Bheema pulled Jarasandha apart, the two halves joined back together seamlessly and he came alive again!

Bheema started tiring. He started to lose hope of ever beating Jarasandha.

Krishna, Arjuna and Yudhishthira were watching the match. Bheema turned and looked in despair at Krishna for help.

Krishna, always the strategist and the one with the master plans, came to his rescue immediately. He picked up a blade of grass and held it up for Bheema to see.

Then he pointedly tore it into two halves lengthwise…

He put the opposite ends together and threw them down.

Bheema was quick to get the message!

He tore Jarasandha's body in two halves, as Krishna had said, and flung the halves down with the opposite ends together.

The two halves could not unite.

And that was the end of Jarasandha, the supreme ruler of the Magadha empire!

He met his end because he took to unfair and cruel ways, and troubled the other kings, even threatening to kill them. So, I suppose he had it coming…

Jarasandha attacked Mathura no less than seventeen times. The eighteenth time, Krishna, fed up with Jarasandha's stubbornness, ordered the capital of Dwarka to be built in the midst of the ocean, where none could come. He himself left Mathura and went away to Dwarka to avoid battle with Jarasandha.

KAUSHIKA, THE MIGHTY KING WHO BECAME SAGE VISHWAMITRA

In the olden days, there lived in our country very learned and wise men. They were called rishis or sages. They did many years of *tapasya* or meditation and gathered great powers.

And how did they do that? Well, when they did *tapasya* they could control their breath so perfectly that they could even stop breathing completely.

They could go without food for years.

They could control their thirst for as long as they liked.

They could stand on one leg for a thousand years and more.

And all this while they chanted the name of the god they especially wanted to please. And because they practised all these very difficult things, they came out of their penance very powerful indeed!

They shone with a new radiance, lived much longer, could foretell the future, and became supremely strong, both mentally and physically.

They were held in great awe because of their learning and knowledge. Even the most powerful kings trrrrr...embled in front of these mighty rishis and bent over backwards to please them!

Usually, these rishis went away to remote woods or to quiet mountains to do their penance. They built their ashrams or hermitages in serene glades in the forest and spent their days in silent meditation. They also taught young students and princes the art of war, and the Vedas and scriptures. They visited the courts of kings when invited and advised them on pressing problems related to governance. The rulers gave them a royal reception and listened carefully to all that they said.

There were several sages, such as Bharadwaja, Vadhula, Badarayana, Bhrigu, Gautama, Atri, Kutsa, Kashyapa, Angirasa, Shandilya, Kaundinya, Matanga, Yagnavalkya, Kanva and many more! Of these great rishis, some were gentle in nature and humble. Most were quiet and spoke very little. They thought more and said less, you see. Just the opposite of what we often do!

Some were rather ferocious and could get angry very quickly indeed. Like the sage Durvasa. All the rajas and maharajas of those days quaked before him! They took great care to keep him happy whenever he visited them. He could curse at the drop of a hat… er…well, *jata*.

Some were quiet, wise and gentle. Like sage Vashishtha, who was the adviser and *rajguru*, or royal priest, at the court of king Dasharatha.

Some were very short but very powerful, like the sage Agastya; or short-tempered, like sage Vishwamitra, who bridled at the smallest thing. He flew off the handle quite easily! And, because he spoke or cursed before he thought, he often regretted it. Because of his infamous quick temper, his power of penance got spent.

You see, that was like his bank balance: every time he did his *tapasya*, the amount of '*tapas* power' or '*tapobalam*' went up. And every time he lost his temper, his *tapobalam* plummeted! (I think we are just beginning to see why we should not lose our temper very often!)

This story is of two very powerful rishis; one of whom was quite jealous of the other!

But why was that?

It was because one seemed to have many more powers than the other, even though he was very quiet and spoke little, while the other worked very hard and did a lot of *tapasya* to become even more powerful. However, he was quick-tempered and got into a huff very easily!

Yes, you guessed right! This was a competition between sage Vashishtha and sage Vishwamitra!

It all began when the sage Vishwamitra was not a rishi at all.

He was the great Kaushika Maharaja, the king of a large and formidable kingdom! He won many battles and added to his territories time and again.

Unfortunately, he was also very proud, arrogant and impatient. They had to listen to him, or he would punish them. He could not stand anyone who spoke otherwise. He had a raging temper, which got the better of him very often.

But one fine day…everything changed!

How?

Shall we find out?

That day, the great Kaushika Maharaja was out in the forest with his huge entourage of soldiers. They had wandered about for a long time and were very tired and thirsty. They looked around for a shelter to rest their weary limbs.

The maharaja's men went scouting around. And what did they see but this beautiful ashram nestled among the trees in the woods! They went back and reported their discovery to their king.

'Your highness,' spoke one weary soldier, his hand on his heart, to show his respect and loyalty to his king. 'We looked around and found this secluded ashram in the forest!'

'Yes,' said his companion, 'it is beautiful and serene. There are big, shady trees, filled with birdsong.'

'My lord,' said the first, 'I think it must be a rishi's hermitage. We can ask him for permission to rest there for a while.'

'Well, what are we waiting for?' said Kaushika Maharaja in his rather haughty manner. 'I am sure he will agree.' So he strode regally to the ashram with his retinue of attendants.

In those days, it was normal for the kings to go hunting, as a sport. The rishis offered shelter to them as they respected the kings. The kings were also very courteous to the rishis.

It was sage Vashishtha's ashram. When he heard that Maharaja Kaushika had arrived, he came out to welcome the king.

'O great king, I am indeed honoured by your visit!' spoke the sage politely. 'Please tell me how I can serve you. Do treat my simple abode as your own!'

Kaushika Maharaja was pleased.

'O sage Vashishtha,' he said, 'my soldiers and I are exhausted and thirsty! We would like to quench our thirst and rest for a while. Then we shall be on our way!'

'But, of course,' said the kindly sage, 'nothing would please me more.'

The rishi went into his hermitage and within a few minutes, huge pitchers of water arrived for the king and his soldiers. They all drank their fill and washed up. The soldiers felt much better and so did their king.

The sage smiled kindly and said, 'O king, food will arrive in a few moments. After that you can rest your weary limbs in my ashram before you return to your palace!'

'I would not want to trouble you, O sage,' said the king. 'In this simple hermitage, it will be difficult for you to feed my massive army. You have made us feel much better. I think we should take our leave now!'

'Oh no, O king, it's no trouble at all!' said the soft-spoken sage, smiling. 'It is, in fact, my pleasure!'

And wonder of wonders, in no time, h-u-g-e platters of food and fruits and sweets were placed in front of a surprised king and his soldiers.

They ate to their heart's content. By the time they finished, their stomachs were quite ready to burst!

As the men felt drowsy after the royal meal, rolls of bedding also arrived for them to rest on!

Kaushika Maharaja was very pleased. And he was rather amazed too.

He wondered, 'Hmm…how could this rishi, living in a humble hermitage in the lonely forest, provide such a fine feast for hundreds of my soldiers? That too within moments?'

Finally, he could not control himself. He just had to find out!

'O wise one,' said he, 'how is it that in this simple hermitage, where there is no grand kitchen or help, you were able to feed me and my massive army? And that too with such delicious food? And so quickly too. I am wonderstruck!

'I, a king…' he continued, 'and the master of a vast kingdom, with thousands of attendants at my command, could not have done half as well!'

'My dear king,' said the sage diplomatically, 'it was a great pleasure to serve you and your army.'

'Yes, but how…?' pressed the king, wanting to get to the bottom of the mystery.

'Well,' the sage revealed, 'I have the celestial Kamadhenu with me. She is a gift from Lord Indra. She can provide me with anything I ask for, in the blink of an eye!! I just have to request her, that is all!'

The king was dumbfounded. 'You mean all this came from the cow called Kamadhenu? I cannot believe it!'

'It is quite true, O king!' replied the *rishi* calmly. 'In this simple hermitage she answers all my basic needs, as I devote my time to my yagnas and holy rituals.' Kaushika Maharaja was not happy at all. His thoughts took a new turn. 'Why should this simple man, living in a hermitage, need this amazing animal? Its place is in my royal palace! I have to feed and look after thousands every day. I have to host royal guests. Most definitely, this miraculous cow will be more useful there!'

He turned to the rishi. 'My dear sage,' he said, 'I am indeed very thankful for the wonderful welcome you gave us. But I do feel that you have no need for this magical cow in your hermitage. It is certainly needed more in my kingdom.'

The rishi was rather surprised at the king's audacity, but he spoke politely, 'She belongs here, O king! But if you feel very strongly about it, I shall not stop you.' Sage Vashishtha was very wise and generous. He also knew that Kaushika Maharaja was blessed with a very short temper indeed, so he thought it better to not start an argument with him.

The king was a little surprised when the sage gave in so easily. He ordered his soldiers to go and fetch the wonder-cow, Kamadhenu.

The men left to carry out the king's orders. But they soon found that Kamadhenu was no ordinary cow!

One of the soldiers took hold of the rope that tethered her to a peg and tugged at it. Kamadhenu would not go with him. The man pulled harder. The cow refused to budge!

He went and reported this to his king.

Now the king himself walked to the cowshed. He grabbed the rope and tugged at it. Kamadhenu held her ground.

We all know that Kaushika Maharaja's temper sat on the tip of his nose. He was very offended indeed! A gentle little cow – how dared she defy him, a maharaja? How dared she refuse to go with him? He yanked at the rope roughly.

The cow shook her head. The next instant the most amazing thing happened!

Out of the cow's body poured out hundreds and hundreds of armed soldiers, dressed in shining armour, carrying swords and bows and arrows. They fought the king's soldiers fiercely!

Within no time Kaushika Maharaja's large and powerful army was defeated. Not a single soldier was left standing.

Kaushika Maharaja could not believe his eyes. This was not possible! He thought he was having a bad dream! A nightmare!

Trembling with rage and disbelief, the king glared at the sage.

Sage Vashishtha was standing aside, watching everything quietly. He spoke, 'O king, I warned you that her place is here. But you would not listen!'

'How dare you?' roared the livid king. 'How dare you do this to me, the great Kaushika Maharaja… you, an ordinary rishi!

'Do you know how powerful I am? Do you know how many kingdoms I have conquered?' the king continued arrogantly. 'And now, a mere cow has defeated and killed my large army! You will pay for this, O rishi.'

He turned on Vashishtha. 'Let us see now how powerful you are. Let us fight each other. We shall see who wins!' The king was so angry that he forgot how kind and hospitable the sage had been to him and his soldiers. He had offered them shelter, rest and the most delicious food.

The king whipped out his bow and arrows. He, the all-powerful king, was not going to be outdone by a frail little hermit!

He knew no fear. He was the conqueror of the world!

If this puny rishi thought too much of himself, he would teach him a lesson he would not forget in a hurry.

Sage Vashishtha saw that the king was in no mood to listen to reason. The rishi tried to calm him down, but the king would not listen.

Realizing it was futile to reason with the king, the sage sat down quietly and closed his eyes in meditation. He offered no resistance. He did absolutely nothing to stop the king.

The king was bewildered. 'Are you not going to defend yourself, O rishi?' he mocked the sage. 'Are you going to give up your life without a fight?'

The sage did not answer. He seemed to be in deep meditation. He placed his Brahma *dandam,* the holy stick endowed with magical powers, upright in front of him!

This angered the king all the more!

All was quiet.

'Well, don't say I didn't warn you!' said the king and released an arrow from his bow. It twanged off and flew precisely towards the target. The king was an excellent marksman and the hero of many a war!

No sooner did the arrow approach the sage than it was swallowed by the Brahma *dandam*!

The king was taken aback.

He launched another arrow. The Brahma *dandam* swallowed this arrow as well!

The king could not believe his eyes! He nocked another arrow and shot it off...then another...and another...

'Take that,' he said, 'and that, and that, and that...' He let loose a shower of arrows, but the

Brahma *dandam* gobbled up all of them! None of them so much as touched the sage, and he continued his silent meditation.

The king's anger knew no bounds. He felt insulted as a master archer. He began to use his mighty divine arsenal. He closed his eyes, recited mantras and sent the weapons whizzing in sage Vashishtha's direction.

But none of them could get past the Brahma *dandam* planted in front of the sage. At last, the king unleashed the Brahmastra, the most powerful weapon of all, capable of annihilating the enemy.

Lo and behold! That too disappeared into the Brahma *dandam*!

Kaushika Maharaja could no longer take this humiliation. He had been thoroughly defeated; crushed by the simple stick called the Brahma *dandam*!

'What's the use of my kingly power and all my learning in the art of war?' he thought bitterly. 'Of what use is my skill at archery and my Kshatriya strength?'

At that moment, his belief in himself was blown to smithereens.

'*Dhik Kshatriya balam! Brahma tejo balam, balam!*' he exclaimed in Sanskrit!

(Fie! The strength of the Kshatriya! The only strength [worth having] is the strength of the Brahma power. The knowledge of the Brahman, the supreme knowledge!)

Which was what sage Vashishtha possessed thanks to all his penance and meditations!

And do you know what Kaushika Maharaja did?

Right there and then, he immediately threw down his weapons and renounced his kingdom, his power, his armies and his wealth. He donned the clothes of a mendicant and walked away into the forest.

'I shall be a king no more,' he declared. 'I have no use for the powers of a Kshatriya! If a rishi can do what a powerful king cannot, then I would rather become a rishi.'

Then he took a vow: 'I promise to myself, this moment, that come what may, I shall achieve

the power of a Brahmarishi! A possessor of supreme knowledge!'

He lived in the forest, ate only fruits and roots, and performed penance for a thousand years.

At long last, pleased with his devotion, Lord Brahma appeared before him, and blessed him with the title of 'Rajarishi', which means 'a king who has turned into a sage!'

But that alone did not satisfy Rajarishi Kaushika! He had set out to become a Brahmarishi, and didn't want to settle for anything less. He sat down to do *tapasya* for several millennia more. The heavens trembled with the austerity of his penance!

Indra, the lord of the heavens, became fearful of losing his throne and power! What if the king gained supreme power through his *tapasya*? What, then, would happen to him, Indra? He might lose his place in Indraloka!

No, he decided, that could not – and must not – happen! He would not allow that if he could help it. He would have to stop this very determined king. So, he sent one of his beautiful divine dancers, Menaka, to charm the *rajarishi* out of his *tapasya.* And he succeeded. Kaushika fell in love with Menaka and broke his *tapasya*.

However, after a while the *rajarishi* realized his mistake and repented. He went away yet again for another millennium of penance. Brahma was very pleased with the determination of the *rajarishi* and gave him the title of 'Maharishi'!

But was Maharishi Kaushika pleased? No, not too much!

Brahma told him that he could become a *Brahmarishi* only when he would overcome his anger and his passion. Well, Maharishi Kaushika was not one to give up easily at all.

Once again Indra sent another beautiful *apsara*, Rambha, from his court, to distract Maharishi Kaushika! The *maharishi*, furious at being interrupted again, cursed her and went away to the Himalayan mountains to perform severe penance.

He stopped his breath almost completely and fasted for another thousand years. He sat in deep meditation, in quiet concentration. Years passed. He did not stir! He forgot hunger and the needs of the body. At the end of the penance, when he opened his eyes, he was shining with a new radiance and grace.

Just as he was about to break his fast with a handful of rice, Indra appeared before him in the guise of a beggar. This was also a test. He asked for the rice that

Kaushika was about to eat. The *maharishi* instantly gave it to him! He had overcome hunger completely. He had overpowered anger and pride.

Lord Brahma stood before him, thoroughly pleased with his achievement.

'O sage,' said Brahma, 'you are no more the king I have known! You have risen to become a *rajarishi* and then a *maharishi*! Now you have surpassed and conquered yourself. You are a *jitendriya*, one who has conquered his senses! You are now a *Brahmarishi*!

'From now on you will be known as "Vishwamitra" – the friend of the world!'

Vishwamitra humbly thanked Lord Brahma.

But there was one more task to be done. His conqueror – the sage Vashishtha – had to accept him as *Brahmarishi*, otherwise his penance would be incomplete! He went to sage Vashishtha, who warmly welcomed him and said, 'My friend, you are truly a *Brahmarishi* now!'

And that is how Maharaja Kaushika became the great and glorious sage Vishwamitra! In his new role, he had great compassion for *everyone* who came to him for help.

But, yes, you guessed it, he was given to sneaky little bursts of temper!

Now let us see how sage Vishwamitra is connected to the historical name of our country? To him and the apsara Menaka was born the princess Shakuntala, who in her turn married king Dushyanta. And to them was born prince Bharata, who became a great emperor when he grew up. It's after him that our country is named Bharata!

KING NALA, THE GREAT HORSEMAN AND AMAZING COOK

This is the extraordinary story of a great king called Nala, who ruled over the kingdom of Nishada. He had great knowledge of horses and was adept at horse riding. A fearless warrior, he was a fair and just ruler of his kingdom. Besides being handsome, he was blessed with humility and great compassion for all humanity.

We might say that we've heard of kings who possessed many of these characteristics. True! But then king Nala had another amazing quality. Which perhaps no other king has ever been known to have. And what do you think that was?

Well, he was an extraordinary cook! He even wrote a book on cooking called *Paka Darpanam*.

Paka means cooking and *darpanam* means mirror; therefore the title means 'the mirror to cooking'. It is believed to be the first cookbook to have ever been written!

In this book he includes a vast variety of recipes – vegetarian and non-vegetarian, curative, exotic, ayurvedic, fasting and feasting foods, and many, many more. There are appetizers, sweets, savouries, fruit recipes, juices, laxatives and treatments for various stomach conditions, both nourishing and toxic foods – and how to use them to the best effect, as well as foods for restful sleep and peace of mind! Very comprehensive, indeed!

He also talks about the right way to serve and partake of food. He describes the qualities of an excellent host and an ideal guest.

If there was one weakness Nala had, it was his love for the game of dice. What made it worse was that he was a very poor player of the game. And, as it happened, it completely transformed his life and fate.

This is how it happened…

Nala was busy ruling his kingdom, expanding his empire and doing all that every good king did.

One day, he was sporting in his royal gardens when he caught hold of a beautiful swan. The frightened bird, thinking that the king would kill it, pleaded for mercy, saying: 'O King Nala! O great ruler of the Nishadas! You are famed for your wisdom, generosity and kindness. If you let me go, I will be eternally grateful…

'And, O king, I'll carry your glory and praise to the very beautiful Damayanti, the daughter of Bhima, the king of Vidarbha!'

'I had no intention whatsoever of killing a lovely bird such as you!' said Nala. 'Do carry my message of love to princess Damayanti...tell her I long to see her...'

And the swan flew to the kingdom of Vidarbha and into the palace gardens where Damayanti strolled, gathering flowers and admiring the beauty of the birds.

'O Damayanti! My virtuous and charming princess, whose beauty is unparalleled! What I have to tell you will hold you enraptured...for I speak of none other than Nala, the great ruler! Nala, the valiant, powerful and handsome king of the Nishadas, unparalleled in bravery and strength – and an exceptional cook, to top it all. You cannot help but fall in love with him if you know of him!'

'Oh, indeed!' said the surprised Damayanti. 'Do tell me more, my sweet bird, about this paragon among men.'

'I'll be happy to, my princess, for there is no man more worthy of your hand as Nala!' continued the swan. 'He is unbeatable in battle, unmatched in his skill with horses, handsome and strong beyond compare, honourable and kind-hearted, and very humble too. To cap it all, he is a divine cook!'

So went on the swan, praising Nala to the princess until she was quite sure that she wanted to marry this great king with whom she felt she was already in love.

The swan flew back, carrying her wishes to Nala. The king decided that he would win the beauteous Damayanti's hand and marry none other…

The day of the *swayamvara* came when Damayanti was to choose her husband.

Kings came from far and near to the kingdom of Vidarbha, having heard tales of the beauteous and virtuous Damayanti.

Nala too set out for the event. He was already deeply in love with Damayanti.

Now the story took an unexpected turn.

Not only had the kings gravitated to Vidarbha, but devas had also descended to earth, eager to win Damayanti's hand.

Agni, Indra and two other devas set forth for the *swayamvara*…

On the way, who did they meet, but king Nala! They asked him where he was headed. When he said he was going to Vidarbha, they asked him for a favour.

'In that case, please be our messenger and carry our best wishes to the beautiful Damayanti. Tell her we're here and eager to win her hand!'

'Oh,' spoke Nala, 'but that will conflict with my own interest, for I intend to win Damayanti's hand myself in marriage.'

'Sorry, young man!' chorused the devas. 'We declared our intent first. So ours is the first choice.'

Nala, being very fair in his dealings, felt that they were right. With a deeply saddened heart, he promised the devas that he would not speak of his love to Damayanti but convey their message alone to her.

Then he went to Damayanti with a heavy heart and tried to convince her to marry the devas. But Damayanti loved Nala and Nala alone! She refused to listen to him.

Much as he loved Damayanti, Nala also felt that he had failed in his promise to the devas. Crestfallen, he informed the devas that Damayanti was determined to marry him and no one else.

And do you know what the devas did?

Well! All four of them transformed themselves into lookalikes of Nala and landed at the *swayamvara*. You see, they were celestial beings and had superpowers!

And when the beautiful Damayanti walked out with a garland in hand, to joyfully place it around her dear Nala's neck she found not one, but *five* Nala's sitting there.

Her hands trembled! She stood rooted to the spot! What could she do?

'Oh, dear God almighty! Who is my Nala?
The one I love. The one I want to marry.
Please God, help me! Help me!'

Thus she cried to herself and closed her eyes in prayer.

And the gods spoke to her in silent answer to her prayers...

'Damayanti, remember there are four celestial contenders for your hand. But since you love Nala, they have turned themselves into lookalikes of him to confuse you and make you select one of them. However, you don't have to worry! Just look for the tell-tale signs of devas.

'They will not blink their eyes; they will not sweat; their garlands will not wilt; their clothes will not rumple; and their feet will not touch the ground since they are not of this earth. And now that your job is made easy, go ahead and garland your Nala! All the best!'

So Damayanti looked carefully! She saw her Nala clearly now.

He was perspiring from the heat.

His garland was wilting slightly.

His royal robes were slightly rumpled.

His feet were planted on the ground.

And of course, he blinked his eyes every now and then as all normal humans do.

Damayanti was overjoyed! She thanked the gods for helping her out.

She happily went forward and placed her garland around Nala's neck! There was a loud cheer.

Everyone was happy for the couple. All the kings stood up and sportingly wished them all happiness!

The devas took their original form and blessed the couple!

So, Nala and Damayanti were married in a grand celebration and began a blissful life together.

But was it to last? Sadly, no!

For there was one wily demi-god who was not happy with this marriage. And that was Kali.

'How do I take revenge on Nala?' he thought. 'He is virtuous, wise, generous, compassionate and a great king. And, to add to that, a superb cook and skilled charioteer with unparalleled knowledge of horses!'

It took Kali all of twelve years to find a chink in Nala's armour of virtue and purity of nature and intent!

Finally, however c, he was able to find that chink. He snapped his fingers. He had hit upon the very idea.

'He has a weakness for the dice – and he is hopeless at it!' he chortled.

Well! To cut a long story short, Nala was lured into gambling his kingdom away to his brother Pushkara.

And soon he and Damayanti lost all they had and had to go away to the forest.

Damayanti advised Nala to take this setback in his stride, but Nala was unable to come to terms with the dreadful turn their life had taken. In the days that followed, Nala sank into deep remorse. Daunted by what the future held for him and unable to face it, one night, he left a sleeping Damayanti and walked away.

Making his way through the dark forest, he came across a ferocious serpent called Karkotaka. It had been caught in a raging fire. Brave and compassionate as always, Nala jumped to its rescue. While he was rescuing the snake, it bit him.

The poisonous bite of the snake turned Nala into a dark, stunted dwarf. No more the handsome, tall and strong-bodied Nala, he took on the name of Bahuka.

'Don't worry, Nala, my king,' said the snake. 'Forgive me for biting you, but your new form will help you move incognito! No one will be able to recognize you as the Maharaja Nala!

'Take my advice, O Nala! Go hence to King Rituparna of the Matsya kingdom! Be his charioteer and the caretaker of his stables. He will be delighted with your expertise with horses and pleased with your magical hand at cooking…

'And above all, from him you can learn the skill of playing the dice. He is proficient at it.'

'I shall forever be thankful to you, O Karkotaka! I shall do as you say!' bowed Nala.

'Take this celestial garment with you. The moment you need to change back to your original form, put this on. You will transform from Bahuka into Nala!' So saying, the snake handed him a robe.

Nala found work under King Rituparna as his charioteer and groom for the royal horses. Nala's culinary skills also helped him become quite the king's favourite.

Meanwhile, Damayanti had been left to fend for herself. She sent her children back to her father, King Bhima of Vidarbha. She roamed around, desolate and forlorn.

She finally found employ with the queen of Chedi, as her lady-in-waiting. She took on the name of Sairendhri.

The queen was very kind to her. She sympathized with Damayanti's predicament and helped her by sending secret emissaries to find out where Nala was.

One royal spy returned with the news of an amazing cook called Bahuka in King Rituparna's kingdom.

Damayanti was an intelligent woman, and she put two and two together. She sent a cryptic puzzle to Rituparna to confirm Nala's presence. In it, she also indirectly conveyed her intent to get married to the next eligible person.

Bahuka was taken aback by this.

He had left Damayanti in the most irresponsible manner. He was now fraught with guilt for his cowardly behaviour. He realized that he still loved her dearly and didn't want to lose her after all.

Taking Rituparna with him, he drove the chariot like the wind to the kingdom of Vidarbha, where Damayanti had taken residence now.

He donned the celestial garment that Karkotaka had given him. He was instantly transformed into the handsome, strong Nala of before. The speed with which he drove the chariot, brought out the Kali from within him. Nala felt himself surge with new energy and confidence.

He invited Pushkara to a game of dice.

Nala, an expert at it now, having gained advice from King Rituparna in the intervening years, tempted the greedy Pushkara into betting his kingdom on the fall of the dice. Pushkara fell into the trap.

Nala defeated Pushkara and won back his own kingdom.

His sense of the fairness did not desert him, though, and he returned Pushkara's kingdom to him.

And, thus, Nala and Damayanti were back together and reunited with their son, Indrasen, and daughter, Indrasena. And, yes, they lived happily ever after.

I have a feeling that Nala would have given up his fondness for games of dice after that. And even if he did indulge in it once in a while, he would have always won!

What do you think?

Nala could drive the chariot like the very wind! When Rituparna asked Bahuka to teach him charioting, Bahuka, in turn, asked him to teach him the game of dice. And that is how Nala was able to defeat his brother Pushkara at the game and redeem his kingdom.

KRISHNA AND SUDAMA – THE EXTRAORDINARY FRIENDSHIP BETWEEN A KING AND A PAUPER

Many are the wonderful stories we have heard of great friendships. Friendship is the most marvellous thing. Friendship builds bridges. It has nothing to do with money or power. It has nothing to do with being rich or poor. Or black or white. Or prince or pauper.

The most unlikely of people become friends in this world. And this is not just true of now, but since time immemorial.

Such a one was the friendship between Krishna and Sudama.

One was a king – wealthy and powerful; the other a pauper. And yet their lifelong friendship stands as an example to all, even to this day.

Well, how did they become such close friends?

Lord Krishna and Sudama's friendship went very, very far back…right to their carefree childhood when, along with others of their group, they got up to a lot of mischief. Krishna was, of course, famous for his pranks. Sudama was the quieter one.

As is often the case in friendship, opposites attract.

Krishna, as we all know, was a Yadava prince, while Sudama was very poor. They went to study with the same guru, the rishi Sandipani. In those days, all students who aspired to learn were admitted into *gurukul*s. So, Krishna and Sudama together learnt the various arts, studied the scriptures and served their guru with great humility.

In the course of time, Krishna ascended the throne of Dwarka, while Sudama spent his time in the study of the scriptures, the teachings of the Vedas and the performance of religious duties.

Being a king, Krishna lived in great luxury in a palace. Sudama, on the other hand, lived in a small hut. The work that he did could not fetch him enough money. His family lived in extreme poverty. They had scarcely enough to eat or decent clothes to wear.

Time went by.

There wasn't a day when Sudama would not think of Krishna…

'My dear friend Krishna...what wonderful times we had! I thirst for the sight of him. Just to see him once would be enough.'

There was not a day when his wife, Susheela, did not urge him to go and visit the friend of his childhood days. There was very little food at home on most days and, at times, their children went hungry as well. Susheela could not bear to see that.

Much against her will, she wished that her husband could get help from his friend. 'You don't have to *ask* him for anything,' she implored Sudama. 'Just a look and he'll understand. Please, won't you go and meet him?'

'Susheela, I do want to see him,' Sudama replied, 'but I could not for the life of me ask him for help. It would be an insult to our friendship. I can't work up the courage to go and meet him. Look at me. Not a shred of decent clothing. And I can't go to him empty-handed, Susheela. I've to carry a gift for him. He's the lord of Dwarka.'

However, after much persuasion, Sudama agreed to visit his old-time friend.

Susheela scouted in her little kitchen until she found some leftover beaten rice (*poha*). She packed it into a small pouch and handed it to Sudama.

'Here you are,' she said, smiling. 'Now you don't have to feel bad about going empty-handed. Don't worry, your friendship will stand the test of this beaten rice; please believe me, my dear husband.'

Sudama set out with a heavy heart…he was nervous indeed. He went halfway down the road and returned home.

'Susheela, please don't force me,' he pleaded. 'I simply can't bring myself to go and see my friend. He is now the ruler of a vast kingdom. It would be improper…'

But Susheela would have none of it. 'What are you afraid of, tell me. You've been wanting to see him all these years, remember? Now is the time.'

Sudama had no answer to that. He reluctantly retraced his steps towards Dwarka. He was torn between dearly wanting to meet Krishna, his childhood friend, and dreading to meet Krishna, the king.

'One should never ask a friend for help…' he told himself, 'it will ruin our wonderful friendship.' And then he thought, 'But, if I expect nothing, then what is the harm in meeting my dear friend?

'But poor Susheela and our children could do with some help…' Lost in these conflicting thoughts, Sudama lost all idea of time and distance. At long last, weary from walking, he found his way to the Dwarka *adhipati* Krishna's palace.

Sudama stood amazed at the sight of the ornate gates and the lush gardens of the palace. The armed Yadava guards at the gates were even more daunting. For a moment, he was seized again with the desire to turn around and head back home.

The guards looked at the poor figure in ragged clothes with surprise and wondered why he was there.

'Just a minute, sir,' said one. 'We can't let you in. Our lordship is busy.'

'What business do you have with the king?' demanded another, wondering what a mendicant could possibly have to do with the ruler of the kingdom.

'Krishna is a very dear friend of mine. I would be much obliged if you would let me see him just once. I've walked a very long way to see him. Kindly – '

'Oh, sure! Our lordship has lots of "friends" like you dropping by to see him every day,' laughed the first guard.

'Ha-ha ha-ha ha!' joined in the other.

Realizing that he was not welcome, Sudama turned to leave.

At that very moment, he heard footsteps hurrying to the gate. And who stood before him but Krishna himself.

'Sudama! Sudama,' cried Krishna in joy, instantly recognizing his childhood friend. 'My Sudama. How are you? How have you been?' Tears flowed down Krishna's cheeks as he beheld his friend's sorry state.

The guards could hardly believe their eyes as they saw their king embrace the poorly dressed man with great warmth and affection. Krishna gave them a stern look of disapproval and they hung their heads in shame.

Krishna put his arm around his friend and led him into the palace.

With deep affection, Krishna sat Sudama down on the royal swing, seating himself on the floor at Sudama's feet, while attendants fetched scented water and an ornate stool for Sudama to rest his feet on.

Krishna lovingly washed his friend's feet, calloused and grimy from his long walk, all the while recalling their childhood days together.

'Remember, Sudama, one day when Guru Sandipani sent us to fetch firewood from the nearby jungle, we got caught in a raging storm and lost our way?'

'Yes, I do, Krishna, I do,' cried Sudama, memories flooding back.

'Krishna has not changed one bit,' he thought to himself, amazed. 'How warm and genuine his regard is for me. How silly of me to have doubted him...' he rued.

'And, do you remember, the storm was so terrifying; the winds so strong, and it became so dark that we couldn't return to the ashram...?'

'Yes, I do Krishna, I do...and the next morning our guru sent out a search party of our classmates to fetch us,' completed Sudama, vivid recollections of their *gurukul* flooding his mind.

All the dark years of need, poverty and sorrow seemed to fall off him as though they had never been.

For a long time, the two friends sat and talked and talked, filling up each other on the time they had spent apart.

Long went on the conversation. Rukmini, Krishna's queen, stood behind Sudama, fanning him, smiling at the childlike enthusiasm of the two friends.

And then the most delectable food arrived on gold and silver platters. And what a spread it was. Sudama had never had such a sumptuous meal in his life.

Krishna served his friend himself, indulging him until Sudama felt so full, he was ready to burst.

'Well, my friend, this has been the most unexpected reward of my life,' exclaimed Krishna, echoing Sudama's own thoughts, 'seeing you after all these years… Not a day has passed without my thinking of you, my dear, dear Sudama. But, where's my gift, my friend? Don't tell me you've come without anything for me?' teased Krishna.

He had already seen that Sudama was carrying a small pouch, which he was trying very hard to hide from him. But Sudama could not bring himself to give the paltry gift of beaten rice to Krishna, the king of Dwarka.

'No, no, Krishna, that is not meant for you,' stammered Sudama, in embarrassment, hiding the pouch behind his back. 'It is not fit for you.'

Krishna pounced on the little bag and opened it. And with great enthusiasm he opened it and took a mouthful of the beaten rice.

'Mmmm,' he cried, 'it has been ages since I tasted such sweet beaten rice. Wonderful.'

As he was about to grab another mouthful, Rukmini stopped him. She knew that Krishna, as the Supreme Power, had already blessed Sudama with all that he could wish for, with one mouthful.

With the second mouthful, she was afraid he would wish himself away.

Sudama watched with tears of joy how his friend relished his humble gift. After a fond farewell, he left.

On the way home, he remembered that he had forgotten to ask Krishna for help as his wife Susheela had suggested.

'Oh no. What will I tell Susheela? Have I failed her and our children?' he thought. 'I didn't have the heart to ask Krishna for anything... He was so kind and generous to me. What a great friend I have in him.'

With these conflicting thoughts running through his mind, he walked home, lost in the rapture of having met his friend.

As he turned the corner to his home, he found his house was missing.

He looked around surprised and confused. 'Have I come to the wrong street? Is this not where my hut used to be?'

And then what did he see?

His wife, Susheela, and his children, dressed in silks and precious gems, emerged from a beautiful mansion that stood where their lowly dwelling had been.

'Look, Sudama, isn't this wonderful?' Susheela asked. 'Behold the miracle of your friend, Krishna. He has rescued us from poverty forever. One word from you was all…'

Sudama found his voice at last. Tears of gratitude flowed down his cheeks.

'No, Susheela, I asked him for nothing,' he told her. 'In fact, I forgot about everything else upon seeing him…such was the joy we both felt. We just talked, talked and talked about our childhood, into the wee hours of the night.

'And Susheela, you should have seen the food we shared… Krishna served me with his own hands.

'I was so ashamed to go to him in these clothes…' Sudama looked down at his worn dhoti and was stunned to find his humble clothes had turned to silk. He had been so preoccupied with his thoughts that he hadn't noticed this transformation.

'O Krishna, O Krishna, how small of me to have doubted your friendship,' he said aloud.

Susheela was quiet. She was lost for words. She understood now the bond between her husband and Krishna, the almighty lord. 'Indeed. He is the Supreme Power who knows everything and everyone,' she thought to herself, 'and his kindness and generosity are boundless.'

Well...needless to say, Sudama and Susheela lived happily ever after with their children. They never knew poverty again.

When Krishna and Sudama were students together at the ashram of Guru Sandipani, the two got lost in a forest into which they had gone to fetch firewood. They got caught in a storm. Both were hungry and Krishna asked Sudama whether he had anything to eat. Sudama, ashamed of having only poha *with him, hid it from Krishna and ate it stealthily. Krishna was reminded of that later when Sudama came to meet him, and he fondly ate the* poha *Sudama had brought.*

KING SATRAJIT AND THE INCREDIBLE SYAMANTAKA GEM

When you look up at the moon, make sure it's not Ganesh Chaturthi night, because, according to Indian mythology, whoever looks at the moon on Lord Ganesha's birthday will have to take the blame for someone else's wrongdoing.

When we don't exactly like accepting the blame for the wrongs we *have done*, taking the blame for something we *have not done* is not likely to be very enjoyable, is it now?

So, what was the problem between Ganesha and the moon? We know that Lord Ganesha never did like the moon, because the moon had had the cheek to laugh at him.

Lord Ganesha's birthday falls on the Chaturthi (or the fourth day of the waxing moon) of the Hindu month of Bhadrapada (the month between 15 August and 15 September, according to the Hindu calendar).

And anyone who dares to look at the moon on that night is promptly gets into the little elephant god's bad books. And, to cap it all, has to take the blame for a wrong not done.

Aren't these reasons enough to stay clear of even taking a peep at the moon on little Ganesha's special day? But what if, just by chance, we were to make the mistake of looking at the moon?

Well, not to worry. We can get rid of the bad effects by listening to this story of Satrajit and a wonderful gem called Syamantaka:

When Lord Krishna was the king of Dwarka, there lived in his kingdom a Yadava nobleman named Satrajit. He was a great devotee of the sun god, Surya, and prayed to him every day.

One day, very pleased with his prayers, the sun god appeared before him and told him to ask for a boon. Satrajit was dazzled by the brilliance of Surya. 'My lord, you are so bright that I can hardly look at you; what is it that makes you so dazzling?' he asked with folded hands.

'My friend,' spoke Surya, 'that is the brilliance of the *mani* or gem – a miraculous ruby – that I wear… the Syamantaka. It has powerful magical qualities.'

Satrajit now knew exactly what he wanted.

'My lord. I wish for the Syamantaka gem that you are wearing,' he said. 'May I have it?'

'Well, yes, I suppose so,' replied the sun god. 'Wherever it is, will be a wonderful place to be. Not only that, it will also give you more wealth that you can ever imagine.'

What more could Satrajit want? He was very pleased indeed. He went back to Dwarka and he wore the Syamantaka *mani* often. And every time he did so, he shone as bright as the sun god himself and bedazzled everyone around him.

One day, he went to meet Lord Krishna, the king of Dwarka. Krishna was glad to see Satrajit and was also quite amazed by the Syamantaka.

'That seems to be a wonderful jewel that you are wearing, Satrajit,' said Krishna in wonder. 'For a moment, I thought you were the sun god himself.'

'I got it from Lord Surya,' boasted Satrajit. 'Do you know it gives me loads of gold coins and riches.'

'Oh, that is fortunate indeed,' said Krishna, 'but I do feel that it should be used for the welfare of your friends here in Dwarka, and you should give it to them.'

'I don't think so,' Satrajit was quick to reply, surprised that Krishna should expect him to just give it away. 'After all, it is a reward from Surya for my prayers to him.'

Krishna thought it better to let the matter go and did not pursue it.

Time passed…

One fine day, Satrajit's brother, Prasena, wore the gem to a hunt without his brother's permission. And, of course, because he wore the special ruby, he shone radiantly. The forest lit up with his presence. Unfortunately, a lion saw Prasena, killed him and carried away the Syamantaka.

As it bounded away with the gem, Jambavan, the great and powerful king of bears, saw him. He, in turn, attacked the lion and killed it. He took away the Syamantaka for his child Jambavati to play with.

Jambavan was gigantic, extremely strong and very, very powerful.

Now, how strong do you think he was?

Well, we get an idea of that from the fact that he could grab Ravana, the formidable ten-headed demon king, whom he called the ten-headed 'insect', in his fist and dangle him over his child's crib as a plaything.

That's how mighty he was.

Now, Satrajit found his precious Syamantaka missing. He was shocked. Where was his prized gem? Where was he to look for it?

'Wait a minute,' he said to himself. 'I know exactly who could have stolen it. It must be Krishna. He was the one who wanted me to give it away. The cheek of him!' Without wasting a moment, he set off in search of Krishna.

Krishna was holding court in his palace.

Satrajit went straight to him, raring to fight. 'Krishna,' he shouted, 'I didn't know you would go to the extent of stealing my Syamantaka. If you had wanted it so badly, you could have requested me and I'd have given it to you.'

Krishna was taken completely by surprise. 'What do you mean, Satrajit? Are you implying that I stole it? Of all the lies I have ever heard!'

'Yes, that's exactly what I mean, Krishna,' said Satrajit, sarcastically. 'You have stolen it. And I'll be much obliged if you would hand it over to me.'

'Oh, indeed?' said Krishna, incensed. 'And what proof do you have, my friend?'

'You were the one who asked me to give it away. You've had your eye on it all along,' taunted Satrajit.

'Well...I must congratulate you on your ability to put two and two together and make five,' said Krishna coolly. 'What if I am able to prove otherwise?'

'Ho!' said Satrajit, 'Go ahead, then. Prove me wrong.'

Now Krishna had to clear his name. He had been falsely accused. Nobody likes to be called a thief, do they? Especially as Krishna was very fair and always tried to do the right thing.

So, he set off to look for the missing *mani*.

Krishna searched high and low but could find no trace of the gem anywhere.

He then decided to look for it in the forest. As he combed the woods, he came to the place where the lion had attacked Prasena. He found Prasena lying there, dead.

He followed the lion's tracks and very soon came to a spot where he saw a bear's footprints along with those of the lion.

Very clearly there had been a roaring fight. At some distance, he found the corpse of the lion.

He tracked the bear's pawprints and arrived at Jambavan's cave.

He saw the crib with the baby in it and hanging above the crib was the brilliant Syamantaka. It lit up the whole cave. He also saw the majestic, fearsome king of the bears, Jambavan.

'And who are you, you human?' growled Jambavan. 'How dare you enter my cave without my permission.'

'Well, you have something I am interested in,' replied Krishna politely. 'Now please hand over the Syamantaka to me.'

'Oh, yes? And why should I? Does it belong to you?'

'Well,' smiled Krishna, 'it certainly does not belong to *you*. I know that.'

'Maybe,' roared Jambavan, towering menacingly over Krishna, 'but it is no business of yours. Now, will you leave, or do you need help? I shall be happy to throw you out.'

'I shall be glad to leave – but *after* you give me the Syamantaka, my friend,' said Krishna calmly, planting his feet firmly on the ground.

'Well, it seems to me you won't listen to reason,' taunted Jambavan. 'Do you want to fight me over it? I'll be happy to.' So saying, he charged at Krishna.

'If you want a fight that badly, I'll gladly oblige,' laughed Krishna, not at all daunted by Jambavan.

So they wrestled and fought…

They grappled, rolled and threw each other…

They got back up and locked arms again.

And so the battle went on and on.

It continued for fourteen days and fourteen nights.

Have you ever heard of such a fight?

Krishna, who was quite small in comparison to the great Jambavan, held his ground. He was not in the least tired. Jambavan was quite surprised!

'Not a single human has been able to stand up to me until now,' he wondered in confusion, 'but this one seems to neither tire nor accept defeat. Come to think of it, he seems to be getting stronger by the minute. How is that? There is more to this human than meets the eye,' he concluded.

And then it struck Jambavan that Krishna was no ordinary mortal. He was Lord Vishnu himself.

'Goodness. I have been fighting the lord himself,' thought Jambavan, filled with remorse.

He kneeled with folded hands and said to Krishna, 'My lord, I was mistaken. I have been wrestling with Lord Vishnu himself. You must forgive me.'

'Not at all,' said Krishna, smiling. 'Satrajit blamed me for stealing the Syamantaka. I have to prove that I am innocent. And you know, my friend, you cannot keep what is not yours, anyway.'

'I beg your forgiveness, my lord,' replied Jambavan. 'My might and pride got the better of me. But I shall make it up to you.'

'Just give me the gem so that I may hand it over to the foolish Satrajit,' said Krishna.

'This instant, my lord,' said Jambavan, 'this very instant.' He gave the ruby to Krishna.

When Krishna restored the ruby to Satrajit, Satrajit was deeply ashamed of his mistake. To make up for it, he gifted the Syamantaka *mani* to Krishna, which he refused.

He also gave his sister Satyabhama's hand in marriage to Krishna, which Krishna accepted.

And that brings us to the end of this story.

Now, if you happen to look at the moon on Ganesh Chaturthi, remember that you have just heard the story of Satrajit – and so you are safe.

As a token of respect, Satrajit offered his sister Satybhama's hand in marriage to Krishna which Krishna accepted. Satyabhama was one of the prime queens of Krishna, the other being Rukmini. Being Satrajit's sister, she was also known as Satrajiti.

BHEEMASENA, THE PANDAVA PRINCE WHO HAD THE STRENGTH OF 16,000 ELEPHANTS

Surely you have heard of the five Pandava brothers and their cousins, the hundred Kauravas? They are the heroes of the huge epic, the Mahabharata. They lived, some five thousand years ago, in the grand city of Hastinapura.

The story is a very, very lo…oo…ng one, and that is why it is called the 'MAHA'bharata. Let us pick up *one* thread of the story that will lead us to where we want to go.

To begin with, there were these three brothers, Dhritarashtra, Pandu and Vidura. The first two were born to queens Ambika and Ambalika, wives of the king Vichitraveerya. They were royal princes with a right to the throne. Vidura was their stepbrother, the son of sage Vyasa and Parishrami. He was wise, intelligent and very fair in whatever he did. He was very close to his brothers.

Now, of the two royal heirs to the throne, Dhritarashtra was the elder, but Pandu was the one who got to become king. Why was that do you think?

Well, it was because Dhritarashtra was born blind. Do you suppose he liked his right being taken away? Not at all. So right from then on, he was not too happy with the situation!

In time, a hundred sons were born to Dhritarashtra and his wife Gandhari. They were called the Kauravas and they all became bright young warriors.

Pandu married the beautiful and intelligent princess, Kunti, to whom were born five little princes, who were called the Pandavas. Born of five gods, they were strong, handsome and brilliant. Each one of them was an expert in the use of weapons and the art of war.

The eldest called Yudhishthira, or Dharmaputra, was very kind and always spoke the truth. He got the name 'Dharmaputra' because he was the son of the lord Yama, or Dharmaraja, who decided how long each person should live on the earth. Next came, Bheemasena, called Bheema for short. He was the son of the wind god, Vayu.

Third came Arjuna, the son of Indra. He was an incredible marksman and an expert in the use of the bow and arrow. The youngest of all were the twins, Nakula and Sahadeva. They were wonderful with horses.

Our little nugget here is about the second brother, Bheemasena.

As each of the five brothers was special in his own unique way, what was so remarkable about Bheemasena?

Well, he was very, very, very strong. So strong that – now hold your breath – he could carry all his brothers, together, on his shoulders very easily. He could uproot trees like they were blades of grass. He could scoop up a mountain and hold it up in the palm of his hand. He had the strength of 16,000 elephants in him. Isn't that mind-boggling? His amazing physical might made him proud, and that's what this story is about. This story has to do with Bheemasena's conceit.

One day, while Bheemasena and his four brothers were living in the forest, their wife, Draupadi, asked him to fetch her the lovely flower *parijata*.

Bheema wanted to make Draupadi happy, so he immediately set off to Indra's palace garden, where *parijata* flowers bloomed in abundance. He walked and walked and walked. The garden was truly a long way off.

Just as he was about to enter the beautiful place, he found a huge old *vanara* with his tail right across the path. Bheema was very annoyed. He was tired and cross from travelling for so long and, therefore, not in the best of moods.

'Hey, you old lazybones,' he snapped, 'can't you see you are blocking my way? How do you think I will get across?'

The old *vanara* did not seem to hear him at all. He just sat slouching, mumbling something, with prayer beads in his hand. He did not move one bit.

Bheema called out again, in a louder voice, 'Hellooooooo! Can't you hear me? Are you deaf? I WANT TO GO ACROSS INTO THE GARDEN.'

But the *vanara* didn't move, although he did look up and then down again. He seemed to be saying his prayers.

Our proud Bheemasena was furious by now. How dare this old, frail *vanara* not listen to the great Bheema.

'YOU OLD MONKEY!' he roared. 'YOU DARE TO DISRESPECT ME. DO YOU KNOW WHO I AM? I AM BHEEMASENA, THE STRONGEST OF THE PANDAVA PRINCES. I CAN PICK YOU UP WITH MY LITTLE FINGER AND HURL YOU MILES AWAY.'

The old *vanara* finally raised its head and said in a feeble voice, 'My son, do not get angry. This aged body is too tired to move. Please be kind enough to shift my tail out of your way. Then you can go on as you wish.'

'Hmmmph,' snorted Bheema. 'You could have told me that right at the start.' He bent down and put his hand under the *vanara*'s tail to lift it up. And he heaved. But the tail was surprisingly heavy.

Bheemasena tried again. And harder. He could not lift it even an inch. He was puzzled. He gathered all his strength together and heaved once more, using both hands.

'MMMMMMMMMMPhhhhhhhhhhhhh!'

And again: 'MMMMMMMMMMMMMMM... MMMMMphhhhhhhhhhhhhhhhhh.'

And, then, again: 'UUURRRRRRRRRRRR... GGGGGGGGGGGGGGGHHHHHHH.'

But NO. The tail would not budge. In fact, Bheema's hand was trapped under the tail and he could not pull it out. 'Owwwwwuuuuuchhhhhhhhh!' he yowled in pain.

He felt that there was something very wrong there. How was it even possible that he, the mighty Bheemasena, was unable to lift an old *vanara*'s tail?

Then it dawned on him. This was no ordinary *vanara*.

But who was it? Well, he must definitely be someone very powerful indeed.

Now Bheema felt thoroughly ashamed of himself. He knew that his enormous pride had prevented him from being polite and had kept him from recognizing this extraordinary person.

'I am very sorry, sir,' he said, bowing, 'I was being foolish and rude and haughty. Can you please tell me who you are? I feel you must be a great *tapasvi*, to have such supreme strength.'

The old *vanara* freed Bheema's hand and smiled on him kindly.

'Well, my son, I am Hanuman,' said the grand old *vanara*. 'And, as I too am a son of Vayu, the god of wind, I am your brother as well.'

'Please forgive me, sir,' said Bheema, mortified and feeling rather stupid. 'I was in too much of a hurry, and behaved thoughtlessly.'

'My son, I am old now, and I spend my time here in this beautiful forest of *parijata* trees, chanting the name of Rama.'

Well, then what do you think Bheema did?

He prostrated himself at Hanuman's feet and took his blessings. Hanuman smiled graciously and moved his tail out of the path.

Bheema, having learnt a salutary lesson in humility, was a lot wiser and modest now. He went into the forest and collected a whole lot of the *parijata* flowers for Draupadi.

Look out for the flower mentioned in the story.
The parijata *is a small, sweet-smelling flower with soft white petals and an orange stem. It blossoms to the first rays of the sun in the morning and sheds soon after.*
The story goes that Parijata was a princess who fell in love with the sun god, who left her after a short time to go on his rounds across the sky. She died broken-hearted because of their abrupt parting and was reborn as a flower. And that is why, even as she blooms at the sight of the sun, she sheds in sorrow soon after.

KUMBHAKARNA, THE SLEEPYHEAD PRINCE

You know from the first story in this book that Jaya and Vijaya were the two gatekeepers or *dwarapalaka*s of the abode of Lord Vishnu and they had been cursed with three rebirths on earth. As mortals they would be killed by avatars of Vishnu.

Their first incarnations on earth were as the asuras, Hiranyaksha and Hiranyakashipu. And, as promised, Lord Vishnu had to give them their second rebirths on earth. They were born as the brothers, Ravana and Kumbhakarna.

Most of you have heard of the rakshasa king, Ravana, of whom we read about in the Ramayana. He carried away Sita, who was Rama's wife, to his kingdom, Lanka, against her will. Rama had to fight him to get Sita back. Kumbhakarna tried to intervene to save his brother from disaster and a bloody and destructive battle. But of course, Ravana would not listen.

Let us now take a look at Kumbhakarna, the sleepyhead. Kumbhakarna was born huge. He was called 'Kumbha-karna' because his ears were like pots.

Even as a baby he was always very hungry and greedily gobbled up thousands of living creatures around him, be they human, animal or anything else within his reach. Such was his appetite!

As he grew older, his hunger grew as well. No amount of food was enough for him. If he was not given enough food, he got into a very bad mood. And then heaven help those around him! So, the people in the kingdom took great care to feed him well and keep him happy.

As Kumbhakarna grew older, living things on earth grew more and more scarce. Everyone ran to save themselves from this great guzzler!

What was to be done? Very soon, there would be nothing left on earth. The world would be a vast and empty wilderness…

The people of earth desperately beseeched Lord Indra to save them from this disaster. When Indra eventually confronted Kumbhakarna to fight him, Kumbhakarna attacked him with one of the mighty tusks of Airavata, Indra's *vahan* or mount.

Indra could not defeat Kumbhakarna, so huge was he and so powerful. He was like a mountain. He took huge strides. He looked like a dark thundercloud with flashes of lightning! The earth shook and trembled as he strode on it. He could span the whole world in one stride. He was almost 14,00,000 feet in height. Can you imagine that?

He was also a faithful devotee of Lord Brahma and had prayed to him for many years. Brahma was so pleased that he appeared before Kumbhakarna and told him to ask for a boon.

What would he ask but that the devas be done away with! It's common knowledge that the demons hated the devas. And so, our Kumbhakarna wanted to ask for 'Nirdaivatvam', which means that there should be no gods at all.

Now could Lord Brahma grant that? Of course not.

Gods were important to look after the world. And so, Lord Brahma asked his wife, the goddess Saraswati, to secretly knot Kumbhakarna's tongue. Which she promptly did.

As a result, Kumbhakarna mixed up the vowels and asked for 'Nidrayatvam', which means continuous sleep. Thus, the lord cleverly saved thousands and thousands of lives on earth from Kumbhakarna's insatiable appetite.

Now, Ravana saw that his loving brother Kumbhakarna had been put under a terrible curse. What was the use of the great Kumbhakarna and his mighty powers if he were just going to sleep nearly all his life?

Ravana begged Lord Brahma to let him be awake for at least a short while. And so, Kumbhakarna was granted one day of wakefulness before he fell asleep again for the next six months.

It was during one of Kumbhakarna's long periods of deep sleep that Ravana carried away Sita. Did Ravana heed the wise words of all his well-wishers – his brothers, Vibhishana and Kumbhakarna, and his beautiful wife, Mandodari – all of whom implored him to return Sita to Rama respectfully. No, he did not. And what was the result?

He brought on a huge disaster on his army, his subjects and the kingdom of Lanka. It was only when he saw his army destroyed, his son, Akshaykumara, killed and Lanka set ablaze by Hanuman, that he began to worry. He had not known fear until then.

He thought of his mighty brother Kumbhakarna, who was asleep as usual after a day of wakefulness.

'What is the use of all of Kumbhakarna's strength, if he sleeps when I need him the most?' he grumbled to himself.

'Go.' he commanded his soldiers and ministers. 'Go and awaken the mighty Kumbhakarna, my brother. I need his help now.'

'B...b...b...but, my lord,' they stuttered in terror, 'he has only *just* fallen sleep. He would be furious to be disturbed now.'

'DO AS I SAY!' roared Ravana. 'DON'T STAND THERE GAPING AT ME!'

So, they had no other choice but to wake up the mighty Kumbhakarna.

Kumbhakarna was asleep in his special cave that was decked with flowers, gold and precious gems.

As they approached the cave, a mighty gust of wind blew them away. And immediately afterwards, they were pulled by an invisible force towards the mouth of the cave. There was a mighty rrrr...rrrumbling sound, like a roll of thunder. Whatever could that be?

Well, Kumbhakarna was sleeping. When he slept, he SNORED. It sounded like THUNDER. When he inhaled, the soldiers felt like they were being sucked into the cave, and when he exhaled, they were literally blown away!

This went on for quite some time. It took a lot of effort for them to inch their way to Kumbhakarna's side. He looked like a huge mountain stretched out on its side. His open mouth was like a vast cavern. Each time he snored, everything around him shook and trembled!

The rakshasa soldiers stood around, dithering and wondering how to wake him up. If they did, Kumbhakarna would certainly kill them in a blind rage or eat them up in his hunger. But if they did not, Ravana would most certainly kill them.

They had to obey their king's orders, so they braced themselves.

It was no easy job. Kumbhakarna would not wake up in a hurry and he would be very hungry as soon as he woke up. They brought buffaloes, deer and

pigs. They piled mountains of fruits and many other favourites of Kumbhakarna beside the sleeping giant. He would be thirsty too. So, they brought thousands of barrels of ale, liquor and fruit juices and placed them by his side.

The BIGGEST task still remained…to wake him up.

They began with massaging him with perfumes and oil. They burnt huge sticks of incense, so that he would wake up to sweet-smelling fragrances. That would please him!

They blew huge conch shells into his ears.

They beat GIGANTIC GONGS.

They blew TRUMPETS.

But Kumbhakarna slept on happily. He did not even stop snoring.

Then they all clapped hands together and SHOOK HIM FROM HEAD TO FOOT.

He rolled over to his side and continued sleeping.

They poured BARRELS OF WATER IN HIS EARS.

They climbed on him and JUMPED UP AND DOWN.

But it made no difference to the sleeping Kumbhakarna.

They pulled at his hair. They tickled his feet.

Kumbhakarna, the sleepyhead, slumbered on peacefully.

Now they were very tired of trying to wake him up. They thought of another idea. They rounded up A THOUSAND ELEPHANTS and made them RUN UP AND DOWN ON HIM!

Aha!

Kumbhakarna stirred at long last and opened his eyes!

His eyes were bloodshot with sleep. He was far from happy to have had his sleep interrupted like this. Before he could pounce on them in his hunger and anger, they quickly pushed the huge mounds of food towards him. That kept him busy for a while.

He ate and ate and ate! Then they pushed the ale, liquor and fruit juices towards him.

Kumbhakarna drank and drank and drank!

Finally, his stomach was full, and he was in a good mood!

'WHY DID YOU WAKE ME UP, YOU NITWITS?' he roared. 'YOU KNOW THIS IS MY TIME TO SLEEP, DON'T YOU?'

'B...b...b...ut, my lord...' stuttered the rakshasa messengers, trembling.

'You had better have a good reason or I will make a meal of you in a trice,' Kumbhakarna growled.

'Y...y...yes, my lord. We have been sent b...b...by the king, your b...b...brother.'

'What?' boomed Kumbhakarna. But he was less angry now because he loved his brother dearly.

'Th... th...the king wants y...y...you to come and help him f... f...fight R...R...Rama,' stuttered the messenger.

'Go on, then. Give me the details. And stop stuttering unless you want a wallop from me.'

'My lord... sir...while you were asleep, the king abducted the beautiful princess, Sita, and brought her to Lanka...'

'So? What about it?' demanded Kumbhakarna impatiently.

'Well, she is the wife of the great warrior prince, Rama, and he has come with his *vanara* army to fight your brother Ravana.'

'Oh,' said Kumbhakarna thoughtfully, rubbing his mighty cheek with a huge finger, because, you see, he was really a good person at heart. 'Well, that seems wrong to me. Why didn't anyone tell me about this before?'

'My lord, you were asleep.' said the messengers in a chorus.

'Okay, okay. Now, go away. I'll go and talk to my brother myself,' declared the mighty Kumbhakarna and off he went to Ravana's court.

At the royal court, Ravana welcomed his brother Kumbhakarna with a warm embrace.

'Kumbhakarna, I am so glad to see you,' said Ravana. Kumbhakarna could see that Ravana was very worried.

'My dear brother, what is the matter? You look upset.' He felt that now that he was here, his brother had nothing more to worry about. Nothing was too big for his might!

'Well, that…Rama…is giving me trouble His messenger, Hanuman, destroyed my beautiful gardens and crushed my huge army…'

'Don't worry your pretty heads, brother,' assured Kumbhakarna. 'Now that I am here, I shall put an end to all this trouble.'

'…and he killed Akshaya as well.'

'Good God! We must avenge his death,' roared Kumbhakarna. 'But tell me, first, why did all this happen in the first place?'

'Well, I carried away Rama's wife – ' started Ravana.

'Why on earth did you do that?' interrupted Kumbhakarna. 'You know that is wrong. I suggest you return her with due respect…'

'She is extremely beautiful and fit to be my queen.'

'Maybe,' grumbled Kumbhakarna, 'but you have no business taking away someone else's wife, brother. I hope it's not too late to save our rakshasa race and our beautiful Lanka.

Ravana scowled stubbornly, 'Come what may, I shall not return Sita.'

'Think again, my dear brother,' warned Kumbhakarna. He knew what his brother had done was very wrong. He tried to make Ravana change his mind.

'I know that Rama is a powerful warrior and the incarnation of Lord Vishnu himself,' Kumbhakarna said. 'What you are doing will bring certain death and destruction to Lanka and all its people.'

Kumbhakarna also knew that his brother would not listen to reason. But Kumbhakarna could not let Ravana fight a battle by himself. No matter what happened, he would stand loyally by his brother.

And so it came about that the mighty Kumbhakarna agreed to fight on Ravana's behalf.

What happened after that is a long story, but you should know that our mighty sleepyhead Kumbhakarna fought long and hard but, in the end, he was killed by Rama. No one else had the power to do so.

Thus, Lord Vishnu kept his promise to Jaya and Vijaya, in their second bad birth on earth.

Kumbhakarna, as we know, was the second bad birth of Vijaya in the Treta Yuga, the earlier one being Hiranyaksha in the Satya Yuga. As he was originally one of the dwarapalakas *of Vishnu in Vaikuntha, he was deeply devoted to his lord. Forced only by his staunch loyalty to his brother, Ravana, he reluctantly fought a battle which he did not really want to fight.*

When he fell to Rama's arrow in the battle, he uttered Rama's name before dying. Rama, of course, was the avatar of his beloved lord, Vishnu.

THE SAKYA PRINCE, SIDDHARTHA, WHO BECAME THE MONK, GAUTAMA BUDDHA

What?! Why would a prince want to become a monk? You'll soon find out in this story…

Prince Siddhartha was born to King Shuddhodana of the Shakya kingdom, a warrior clan proficient in the art of war. Siddhartha Gautama was born in Lumbini, now in Nepal, in the fifth or fourth century BCE.

When Siddhartha was still a baby, a wise man prophesied that the king's infant son would grow up to either become a great ruler or a great spiritual master…a leader of people. That made King Shuddhodana wary. He wanted his son to be next on the throne after him.

As a king.

Not an ascetic.

To make sure that his dream came true, he protected his son jealously. The little prince was brought up in royal comfort and in the lap of luxury. Every wish of his was fulfilled. He was sheltered from the miseries of the world beyond the high walls of the palace.

King Shuddhodana had lofty dreams for his son.

He trained his son comprehensively in combat, wrestling, the martial arts and archery. He was destined to be the future king, you see...

However, as much as the prince was adept at these warrior skills and in the study of the scriptures and literature, Siddhartha longed to see the world outside.

One day, at an opportune moment, he slipped out of the palace...

What he saw shocked and saddened him.

He saw...

An aged man.

A sick man.

A dead man,

And an ascetic.

He saw that his life in the palace was not the entire truth. It was not the complete reality.

Life was full of misery and suffering.

A happy and carefree youth led to old age.

Sickness was a part of life too.

And death was the end of life. No one was immortal.

This would all happen to him too one day or the other.

And then there was the ascetic.

He seemed to be at peace despite all the suffering around him.

Why was that? He had to find out.

But how?

Would his father, the king, ever let him leave the palace, in search of truth? Not ever!

And, therefore, Siddhartha decided to leave his life of luxury and riches…

One night, he left his wife, Yashodhara, and infant son, Rahul, while they were asleep, and slipped out of the palace.

And there began the journey of Gautama the Buddha…

He spent years learning from great masters, gaining in knowledge and experience.

He fasted.

He meditated, until he completely lost track of time.

He couldn't rest until he realized the ultimate cause of all suffering. And how to end the relentless cycle of misery. After unceasing effort, he discovered the Four Noble Truths that helped to end all suffering.

He taught the Noble Eightfold Path…

He had finally become the Enlightened One, the Buddha.

He was a man without fear or doubt. He was without anger or want. His mind was as clear as crystal, his heart full of compassion.

However, this story is not just about that...

It is about an interesting incident in his life.

So you want to know what happened on that astonishing day in his life?

Well!

The Buddha was camping one day along with his fellow monks in a forest on the outskirts of a town. As he went on his morning rounds into the town, collecting alms and talking to the people, he found that most doors were closed. He was slightly puzzled at the unusual sight.

As he waited for alms at a doorstep, the householder stepped out and spoke in hushed tones to the Buddha, 'O Venerable One, do not walk the streets of the town! The notorious bandit Angulimala has come into the nearby forest. The residents of this place are now living in terror of him, O Buddha. Please allow me to serve you your meal...do not risk your life needlessly, O Master.'

The Buddha smiled reassuringly at him and said, 'What has he to gain from me? Do not fear for me, my

dear man. I'm completely safe. Besides, I come here, not just to collect alms, but to talk to the people as well and solve their problems in whatever way I can. Rest assured I'm well able to take care of myself.'

'Please do be careful, O kindly Master. He has collected the fingers of 999 of his victims and has strung them into a garland that he wears around his neck. He is waiting to get his final victim to reach his target of a thousand.'

'Fear not, my man,' repeated Gautama, the Buddha. 'I shall take care.' And, having collected his alms, the Buddha walked serenely back into the forest, his heart peaceful, his stride steady, his mind calm and alert. He was also watchful.

He was, as we know, an expert in the martial arts from his days before he became a monk...and was ready for any eventuality.

Soon enough he heard the sound of hurrying feet... fast approaching him.

He knew it was Angulimala.

'Stop, O Monk. There is no escape for you!' spoke the hurrying voice.

Buddha continued to walk, unruffled...

'STOP! I tell you, I can overtake you in no time.'

But Buddha neither hurried, nor stopped. He continued walking at an even and dignified pace, his senses alert. The Buddha's fearless calm and his serene self-assurance angered Angulimala.

'O Monk, do you think I cannot catch up with you?' shouted Angulimala from behind. 'Do you know who I am? I say, *stop right now*!'

Angulimala was surprised that while he had to run to catch up with this monk, the Buddha simply walked at the same placid pace.

'STOP!' shouted the dangerous criminal and stepped right up to the Buddha.

And the Buddha turned and looked at Angulimala with calmness and compassion.

'I stopped long back, Angulimala. What I want to know is – when are you going to stop?'

'What do you mean, "I stopped long back"? You are still walking,' shouted Angulimala angrily.

'I don't mean this stopping, my dear man. I meant, "When are you going to stop what you're doing?" All this waste of lives, this killing? When will you stop that? When will you stop running, Angulimala?' asked the Buddha gently.

The peaceful radiance on the Buddha's face and his eyes filled with kindness told Angulimala that this was no ordinary man.

'O Buddha, don't you see? I couldn't stop even if I wanted to. The world around me is full of hatred and anger. I myself am full of rage. I hate mankind… There is no one who has any kindliness. If I stop, I'll be torn to pieces by people. It is too late, it is too late, don't you see?'

'It's never too late, Angulimala,' replied the Buddha. 'You can stop, now…at this very moment. And there is love and compassion, if you look for it… In the Sangha where I live, there are monks and nuns, full of caring, full of love. Come with me to the Sangha. The Sangha will protect you. I promise…'

Angulimala saw the deep sympathy in the Buddha's face.

He fell at the Great Master's feet.

'Save me, O Buddha,' Angulimala wept. 'I'll follow where you lead.'

And thus it happened that Angulimala, whose actual name was Ahimsaka, became a monk in the Buddhist Order, never to take to violence again!

Strangely enough, Angulimala was earlier a brilliant student at the ancient university of Takshashila. The other students, out of sheer jealousy, set his teacher against him, and the teacher laid the unfair condition upon Ahimsaka, as he was known earlier, to fetch a thousand fingers from willing donors to continue his studies. There was hardly anyone who would part with their finger and, as a result, Ahimsaka took to killing and violence to achieve his target.

THE KING WHOSE MINISTER TOLD HIM, 'EVERYTHING HAPPENS FOR THE BEST'

And then there is this story of the king who had a wise minister who earned his ire for always telling him, 'Everything happens for the best.'

No matter what.

The worst would come to pass and the minister would smile and say, 'Everything happens for the best, O king, believe me.'

Until one day, the king had had enough. He was not in a particularly good mood that day and the minister was getting on his nerves! He was fed up with his minister's platitude and turned his wrathful eye on him…

'Take him away and put him in prison,' commanded the king. 'We'll see what good that does him.'

'My lord, everything happens for the best,' so saying, the minister submitted to being led away to the prison.

After the end of the court that day, the king was just stepping out, when he nicked his finger on a nail on the ornate door to the entrance.

The gash started bleeding.

He had planned to set out on a hunting expedition on that very day. Normally, the minister would have accompanied him. But…

The king was in no mood to allow him go with him on the hunt. 'Let him sit in prison and think it over, the foolish man!' thought he. 'I cannot take his "everything is for the best" line any more.'

The king set off on his hunt along with his attendants.

On his way back after the hunt, the king went looking for some water as he was very thirsty. He found a freshwater stream. He knelt and drank his fill. As he straightened, he was taken by surprise by an attacking tiger.

He knew what he had to do. He lay absolutely still and controlled his breath.

The tiger came close and sniffed at the king – from head to toe.

The king's heart was in his mouth, but he dared not move.

He knew from experience that a tiger would not touch a dead body.

After what seemed a lifetime to the king, the tiger went away.

The king heaved a huge sigh of relief. Thanking his lucky stars for having spared his life, he returned to the palace.

'Let me look in on my minister and see how he is faring,' thought the king, smiling to himself. 'In fact, I would like to hear his opinion about today's incident. I'd like to pick his brain a little on that. Everything happens for the best…bah!'

So he stepped down to the prison cell where the minister was being held and said in a derisive tone, 'Well then, my good man. What do you have to say about today? I got a cut on my finger and while on my hunt I was about to be eaten by a tiger. Now, tell me kindly, how was it all for the best?'

'Well, your majesty,' said the minister calmly, 'the injury to your finger was surely the best thing that happened to you today. Without that you would most certainly have been eaten by that tiger. As you must know, a tiger will not touch an already wounded person...and you couldn't possibly have held your breath forever.'

The king fell into deep thought. He could not but admire the minister's wisdom. But there was yet one more thing, 'I daresay the wound saved my life,' replied the king with grudging admiration, 'so it has certainly been a good day for me, but how does it make the day good for you? You've been languishing in prison...'

'Oh, that. It's most certainly been a lucky day for me, your lordship,' smiled the minister. 'Had you not thrown me in prison, you would have taken me along on the hunt with you and the tiger would most certainly have killed me instead of you because I didn't have a wound on me.'

The king was dumbfounded. He had to accept the profound wisdom of his minister's words. He apologized profusely to his wise minister for having been so inconsiderate. He released him immediately and rewarded him abundantly for his astuteness.

It goes without saying, the minister became one of the king's favourites from that day on.

In those days, the kings encouraged knowledge and scholarship as well as the arts. They surrounded themselves with wise advisers and rajagurus. *They often took criticism and wit from these advisers, in their stride.*

We have the great examples of the Navaratnas in the court of Vikramaditya. We have the legendary example of the camaraderie between Akbar and Birbal.

Birbal was well known for his wisdom and wit and which he very often used to put Akbar right. We have many such stories of Tenali Raman, the poet, scholar and thinker in the court of Krishnadevaraya.

'POR KAI PANDIAN', THE KING WITH A GOLDEN HAND

This story is about an illustrious ruler from the Pandya dynasty who reigned in south India many hundreds of years ago…

Madurai was the capital of the Pandya rulers. It was a city rich in culture and crafts – dance, music and folk arts. It was said that milk and honey flowed there!

In those days, the kings always wanted to stay in touch with their people and know exactly what they thought of their ruler and the way the kingdom was run. If a person were asked to give his honest opinion in the presence of the king, they would have been too scared to speak the truth. So, to get the true picture, the king would often disguise himself as a commoner, cover his head with a shawl or a *chadar*, and walk around in the marketplaces and other public areas where people gathered. He would be in '*maaru vesham*', which is Tamil for 'altered looks' or 'disguised'. He would look like any peasant, merchant or labourer!

Usually, at the end of the day, after nightfall, he would find people discussing the state of affairs, their complaints to each other about injustices and the prices of commodities, among other things. He would stand around listening. At times, he would even take part in the conversations and invite opinions about the king (himself, that is)!

The people would answer unguardedly, unaware that they were talking to the king himself.

The king would then use the information thus gathered in setting right his governance of the people.

One such king was Por Kai Pandian, whose real name we are not aware of. He probably lived about two thousand years ago, between the first and second centuries CE.

As was his wont, one night he was walking around incognito in the streets of the capital city of Madurai when he suddenly heard a woman crying inside one of the houses.

His curiosity aroused, he stopped by the door and listened.

He heard the wife say to her husband, 'O my husband, you'll be away for two whole months for *vyaparam* (trade). Who will take care of me? I will be all alone.'

The husband consoled her, 'I know, dearest, but what can I do? I have to go away on work. But you have nothing to fear. Our king is just and caring. Under his care, no harm will come to you.'

The king was very glad to hear this. It reflected the faith and trust that the people of his kingdom placed in him. He also felt a deep sense of responsibility towards this young wife.

On his rounds, he made it a point to keep a special watch over that particular house.

One day, as he passed by, he heard a male voice inside the cottage. The two months were not yet over, so the husband could not have returned. Fearing that the young wife was perhaps in some kind of danger, and wanting to make sure she was safe, he knocked on the door.

The king recognized the male voice that answered from within and realized with a start that it was the husband, who had returned earlier than expected.

Fearing that the husband might be suspicious of a stranger knocking at his door in the dead of night, the king quickly knocked on all the doors on that street as he passed by them, so that no special suspicion would attach itself to that particular house.

Having done what he could to rectify his mistake, he returned to his palace.

The next morning, the king sat in his durbar to receive his subjects and hear their grievances. There were several issues that came up. The king listened to each one carefully and took just decisions.

At last, one man stood up and said, 'My lordship! Yesterday a very strange thing happened. There was a knock on my front door in the middle of the night, but when I opened it, there was no one there.'

'Oh, indeed?' said the king. 'And who do you think it could have been?'

A buzz could be heard round the royal court.

'Someone knocked on my door as well,' said a second man. 'I too opened the door to find no one standing there.'

'My door too, O king.' said another. 'Someone knocked and ran away before I could find out who it was.'

'How strange, your highness,' spoke yet another. 'There was a knock on my door as well. And when I answered, there was nobody there.'

This went on for a while. The king listened thoughtfully to the complaints.

At last, he spoke. 'So, we need to punish this irresponsible behaviour for sure! What would be the most fitting punishment for such errant behaviour, my people? I want your frank, unbiased opinion. Speak without fear or favour.'

'Cut off the hand that committed the deed, O king,' the people spoke in unison.

'Yes. That will teach the culprit a lesson.'

'Yes.'

'Yes.'

'Yes.'

'We agree.'

So went the chorus among the people gathered.

The king rose to his feet. He drew out his sword from its scabbard and cut his hand off in one sweep.

There was a shocked silence in the court.

People were horrified to see their king's arm dripping with blood.

'Oh, my lord, why did you do this?' they said. 'O dear king, why did you cut your hand off?

'We did not know it was you, my lord.' they cried.

'Yes, but justice cannot be different for a ruler,' declared the king. 'It has to be the same for me and my people.'

'But, your majesty, you must have had a very good reason for doing what you did,' said a man remorsefully.

'Well, yes, there was,' said the king, 'but a punishment meted out by the people should stand the test of justice. Therefore, I cannot forgive myself.'

By this time, the royal physicians had hurried over to attend to the king.

The people requested that the king be fitted with a hand of gold. They wanted nothing less for their beloved and respected king, who did not place himself above his subjects as far as justice was concerned.

And that was how he got the name of 'Por Kai Pandian', which means 'King with the Golden Hand'.

This story is cited as one of the earliest examples of prosthetic surgery, an ancient stream of medicine on the Indian subcontinent. Sushruta is believed to be one of the earliest of Indian physicians, famed for 'rhinoplasty' (what is called a 'nose job' now) to replace the noses of soldiers. Procedures of cosmetic, plastic and dental surgery are found in great detail in his work, the Sushruta Samhita. *Before this, Charaka had compiled the* Charaka Samhita, *containing the very earliest compendium of medicines and medical procedures. India, in its earliest days, was very advanced in indigenous schools of medicine such as Ayurveda and Siddha. Thousands of medicinal plants, their extracts and uses are recorded. Ayurvedic doctors of today follow these treatments even now. Siddha is an ancient stream of medicine that is still in use in some parts of south India.*

QUEEN MEENAKSHI OF MADURAI, ONE OF THE FIRST EVER WOMEN RULERS

This is the story of a princess who became the first woman to rule a kingdom in ancient India.

The practice of having a male heir to the throne to take over the kingdom was prevalent all over the world. So it was for many years in India too.

To beget a male heir to the throne, mighty kings resorted to performing grand pujas, yagnas, prayers, fasts and charity; they also practised Dharma and built temples. In many cases they were granted their wish, as you see in several stories in this book.

But this story is about an unusual case.

The Pandya dynasty was one of the longest lasting and most illustrious of the three main dynasties of south India – the Cheras, the Cholas and the Pandyas – also called the '*muventhar*' or the 'three chiefs'. Establishing their kingdom as far back as the third century BCE, the Pandyas ruled for nearly 2,000 years.

One of the Pandya rulers, Malayadhwaja Pandyan and his queen Kanchanamalai, were without a child for many years and longed for one. The king needed an heir to the throne.

As was the rule in those days, he did all he could to propitiate the gods…with no result for a long time – until he lost all hope.

But finally, after he performed the powerful *putra kameshti* yagna, a girl child of three years emerged from the holy fire in all her glory. She had the brilliance of the moon and the radiant beauty of the sun.

The king was not the happiest with this result though.

He had asked for a son. He got a daughter instead.

Not only that – she was born with three breasts. Definitely not the perfect princess people expected. The king lamented this.

'Who will ever look at this daughter of mine?' he moaned. 'She will the laughing stock of the court…'

A voice from the heavens corrected him:

'O king, she is no ordinary girl. She is destined to be the future ruler of Madurai and a powerful queen. Treat her with the respect she deserves. Teach her the royal arts of war. Skill her in the use of weapons. She will excel.

'Remember too, O king, her third breast will vanish when she meets her equal and her love.'

The king took the words of the prophetic voice to heart.

He trained his daughter, Tadatakai, as she was originally called, with utmost dedication. The princess learnt all the skills of warfare and the use of weaponry brilliantly, putting the most accomplished male warriors to shame. She became proficient in archery and the use of the sword. She grew up and, upon the demise of her father, assumed the reins of the kingdom.

She was brave, fearless and ferocious in her dealings with her enemies. But was she content to rule over Madurai?

No, of course not.

She was both ambitious and daring. When she came of age, she rejected marriage and decided she wanted to conquer the world. She started her

military campaign from the south, going northwards, conquering the kingdoms that she came across.

The devas and Indra, their supreme chief, shuddered at her ferocity and steely determination. She looked at all opposition with disdain.

All who came in her path bowed to her supremacy. No one dared mock her in any way.

Finally, Tadatakai reached the Himalayas and, thence, the mount Kailash.

There she met a young hermit – his hair in a *jata*, ashes smeared on his body, a snake curling around his neck, strong and undaunted by Tadatakai.

Yes, Lord Shiva himself.

She fell in love with him and, instead of fighting him, she declared she wanted to marry him. And lo and behold, her third breast disappeared.

She returned to Madurai along with Lord Shiva, who was henceforth called Sundareswarar. They were married with regal pomp and splendour.

She came to be called Meenakshi, the one with fish-shaped eyes, and ruled Madurai with great competence and intelligence. She won the respect of one and all.

And what a capable ruler she was!

The story of Princess Meenakshi goes very, very far back indeed, to the fourth century BCE. *It is known from lore and verses written later, especially so from a thirteenth-century Tamil epic poem,* Thiruvilayadal. *Movies were also made based on this legendary warrior princess, such as* Meenakshi Thiruvilayadal.

The famous Meenakshi Amman Temple in Madurai, originally built more than 2,000 years ago, was refurbished and rebuilt by generations of Pandya rulers. To date, Meenakshi, the strong and valiant warrior with a mind of her own, who was raised to the status of goddess, is said to rule over Madurai. Shiva, as her consort, is called Sundareswarar. Throughout the year, festivals are celebrated in her honour.

If we look closely, in one of the stone sculptures depicting Meenakshi's wedding, she smiles bewitchingly at her admirers, her right hand clasping Shiva's hand, but tucked on the left side of her waistband is a dagger – a reminder that she is no ordinary woman but a warrior princess and one of the earliest woman rulers in India.

At a time when a princess was married off so she could hand over her right as ruler to her husband, Meenakshi stood her ground and resolutely claimed her birthright.

The main prakara, *or sanctum sanctorum, in the Madurai Meenakshi temple, is dedicated to Meenakshi. Her husband, Sundareswarar, is housed in the consort's sanctorum.*

THE AMAZING YUDHISHTHIRA, WHO ANSWERED THE MOST DIFFICULT QUESTIONS

So here we are, looking into yet another wonderful story in the great epic, the Mahabharata, that takes place during the fourteen-year exile of the Pandava princes. This incident takes place in the thirteenth year of the exile period, the Aranya Parva or the Vana Parva.

The Pandava princes, as we know, were five in all. (Karna was actually the sixth, born first, but could never claim his birthright to his royal lineage. But that is another story...)

It so happened that, while in exile, hunting for food in the forest, the five brothers met a Brahmin priest who came to them seeking help.

He said, 'O young and valiant men, a deer has run away with my tinder sticks. I was just about to light the holy fire for my yagna. Please can you get them back for me?'

'But, of course,' said Yudhishthira instantly, answering for the brothers, 'we are glad to be of help.'

And they pursued the deer. The fleet-footed animal led them on a merry chase through the woods. Its speed was astonishing.

By the time they got hold of the tinder from the deer, Yudhishthira was overcome with exhaustion and thirst. Indeed, all five of them were extremely thirsty.

'Nakula,' Yudhishthira said, 'please would you go and find us some water to drink. I cannot walk a step more, so overcome am I with thirst! After you've had enough, do fill your quiver with water for your brothers too.'

'I shall go this very instant, brother,' said Nakula and was off like a shot.

After much wandering and scouring the forest, Nakula found an amazing lake by a glade of trees – the water was stunningly beautiful and of the purest kind, cool and crystal clear.

Not another creature was in the vicinity except for a beautiful crane – large, magnificent, radiant as the sun and as tall as a palmyra tree.

Nakula cupped his hand and bent forward to drink.

And lo and behold, he heard a voice:

'Do not drink this water, O son of Madri. It belongs to me. You have to answer the questions I pose to you before you partake of it...and then you may take away as much as you require. If you don't answer, there will be dire consequences.'

Nakula was astonished, for there was no one around except the crane. He was much too thirsty to care. His throat was parched.

'Let me have but one sip of water before I bother with this voice of the skies, for I cannot bear a moment of delay,' said Nakula to himself.

And as he took one sip of the nectar-like water, he dropped to the ground, dead!

Yudhishthira, Arjuna, Bheema and Sahadeva waited...and waited...and waited...

When several hours had passed, a worried Yudhishthira sent Sahadeva to look for Nakula.

Sahadeva, after much wandering, reached the same beautiful body of water. He saw Nakula lying there, lifeless...

'Oh, my brother. What has happened to him? Is he dead? Or in a swoon? I have to tell Yudhishthira about this immediately. But let me drink some water to revive myself…' said he and stooped down to drink.

As he did so, he heard a voice from the skies:

'O child, son of Madri. Do not be rash…do not drink this water before you answer my questions, as it belongs to me. You may, after that, drink your fill and take away as much water as you need.'

Sahadeva looked up and around and saw no one. He could hold back no longer, 'Oh, for a few sips of water,' thought he, but no sooner did he take a sip than he fell down dead.

More time passed. The other three brothers, Bheema, Arjuna and Yudhishthira became very anxious.

'O Arjuna,' Yudhishthira addressed his brother, the brilliant archer, 'my fearless and invincible brother. O Dhananjaya, our sole refuge against all enemies at all times, my mind recoils at the very thought of what fate could have befallen Nakula and Sahadeva. I'm truly worried. I depend on you now…'

Arjuna, who was only waiting for his brother's command, jumped up, his bow and arrow at the ready. In his other hand he held a flashing sword.

'This moment shall I go…dear brother,' he said. 'Fear not. I shall get to the bottom of this and I shall bring back Nakula and Sahadeva safely.' He set off instantly to search for them.

Arjuna, Indra's son, had none to equal him in his expertise and accuracy with the bow and arrow. He could shoot in all directions in a split second. He could shoot with equal panache and accuracy with either hand, the left or the right.

As he went, determined to find water, he was all set to find out what had happened to Nakula and Sahadeva. He arrived at the lake at great speed and found Nakula and Sahadeva, lying on the ground.

In that split second, his bow and arrow were in his hands with the speed of lightning, 'Show yourself, O slayer of my brothers!' roared Arjuna like a lion.

Seeing no one, he spoke again, 'Show yourself, if you need to address me, for this is cowardly. My arrows will make a thousand holes in you, ere you can say a word.'

And then he heard the voice in the skies speak:

'Do not act rashly, O Partha. This water is mine. Do not make the mistake of drinking this nectar before you answer my questions, or else you will meet the same fate as your brothers!'

Taken by surprise and not knowing where the opponent was, Arjuna shot a thousand arrows in a trice, covering all directions – the sky and the earth and all in between.

And then, with consummate skill, he shot the *shabda bhedi* arrow – one that could hit the target by locating the precise source of its voice.

Having done what he could to fell the enemy and consumed by thirst, he ran to drink the water…

The voice rang out once more:

'Do not be foolish, O Bharata. You cannot win thus. Once you answer my questions satisfactorily, you may drink the water and carry as much as you require as well.'

Ready to attack the enemy with the left hand, if necessary, Arjuna scooped up the water in his right.

No sooner had he put water to his lips than he slumped to the ground, dead.

Yudhishthira, beside himself with worry at the disappearance of his three brothers and the inordinate delay, turned to Bheema, 'O my brother of immense might and the unparalleled wielder of the mace, I am wracked by worry. I feel something terrible has happened to our brothers. Go without a moment's delay and find out the reason for their disappearance; and do get some water to drink, will you?'

'This instant, brother,' said Bheema, and hastened away in the direction his brothers had gone. Upon reaching the lake, he saw his valiant, invincible brothers lying dead.

He was overcome with great sorrow. Thought he, 'No human hand could have brought down such a one as Arjuna. Each of these men is unconquerable. This must be a magical act. Possibly by a *danava* or a *yaksha*.

'I must go to battle now with my mace, but first I must quench my thirst with a sip of water to revive my energy.' Saying thus to himself, Bheema bent to scoop up some water.

And the voice rang out:

'O child, do not act hastily! This water belongs to me. Answer, first, my questions and then you may drink to your hearts fill and carry back as much as you want.'

Bheema, looking around and finding no one, was too thirsty to care. He put the water to his lips. And he fell to the ground in an instant.

Time passed yet again.

Yudhishthira, left alone and worried beyond reason, muttered to himself, 'I cannot begin to understand what could have happened to my brothers. Each one invincible, brilliant in the field of battle, conquerors of the *daitya*s, the celestial *gandharva*s skilled in the arts of music and dance, the evil rakshasas and all who came in their path; why have they not returned?

'Have they been felled by some unknown magical power? Have they lost their way? Have they, not finding water close by, gone further to look for it?'

'I must find out for myself.' As Yudhishthira set forth in search of his brothers, he was desolate and anxious, and intensely thirsty…

Soon he arrived in the beautiful glade. He was struck by the wonderful surroundings, the quiet, where only the sweet calls of birds rang out. Rare and scented flowers blossomed. The lake looked enchanting.

For a moment he stood there, entranced by its beauty.

And then he saw his brothers lying on the bank, as if in deep sleep, and his sorrow burst forth. He lamented loudly and uncontrollably, tears of grief flowing down his cheeks:

'O mighty brothers of mine. Each one a force unto himself. Heroes of impossible battles. Who could have done this to you? None in this whole universe has the temerity to attempt this. No enemy can stand up to you and none exists whom you could not have crushed. This must indeed be the act of a superior hand. Not human, certainly. Hmm…there is no sign of combat or injury on any of them – they look asleep. No bodily harm has been done to them. 'The water itself seems like nectar...could it be poisoned by Duryodhana, though, the spinner of evil plans?

'No,' he debated with himself, 'if my brothers were poisoned, there would definitely be telltale signs of it. There is no pallor or discolouration of the skin.'

Finally, he came to a conclusion. 'This looks like the work of none other than Yama himself...could it be?'

Thus reasoned Yudhishthira, reining in his sorrow by sheer power of will, schooling himself to think rationally.

And then he descended to the water and as he made to wash himself and drink some water, he heard the voice his brothers had heard but not heeded:

'O son of Kunti. O follower of the path of Dharma. O right-minded and virtuous one. This sweet expanse of water belongs to me. None can drink of it without my permission or answering my questions. O wise Yudhishthira, do not be hasty or else you will meet the fate of your brothers. Answer the questions I ask of you. And then you may drink to your heart's fill and carry with you as much as you want.'

Yudhishthira stopped dead in his tracks. 'Indeed, I cannot take what is not mine. Answer me though – who are you? Who are you that has brought down my mighty brothers, who have never known defeat? Whom neither a rakshasa nor deva, *gandharva* nor

human could bring down? What, therefore, is your purpose in doing so? For they have done you no harm other than quenching their thirst.'

'O fair-minded, Yudhishthira,' spoke the voice, 'I am a *yaksha* through whose prowess your brothers have met their end. Do not be so rash as to commit the same mistake that your brothers did.'

Yudhishthira said, 'You must indeed be more powerful than you admit. My brothers are no ordinary humans. However, I'll not partake of this water until I can fulfil your condition and answer your questions to the best of my ability.'

Thus Yudhishthira, utterly exhausted, deeply saddened and desperately thirsty, controlled himself and submitted to the questions posed by the *yaksha*.

Now, the *yaksha*, knowing the wisdom and fortitude of Yudhishthira, asked of him some very difficult questions indeed. Questions that no lesser person could have answered...

Yudhishthira was immensely patient, wise and humble. He remained calm and thoughtful throughout the series of questions posed by the *yaksha*. As several of them were deeply philosophical, they could be too complex for you to enjoy. But here are a few...

'O Yudhishthira. tell me...

1. What is it that keeps the sun on its course day after day? What makes it rise and set without fail?'

   After thoughtful consideration, Yudhishthira answered:

   'The supreme deity Brahma keeps the sun on its course and makes the sun rise and set unfailingly.'
2. 'How does one attain intellectual greatness and wisdom?'

   'By learning the scriptures, by doing what is right and by serving the aged.'
3. 'Who is alive and breathing and yet not alive?'

   'One who does not think beyond himself. One who is not charitable to the needy, shows no hospitality to a guest, does not respect his ancestors nor himself, is alive and yet not alive.'
4. 'What is it that does not close its eyes?'

   'Fish.'

5. 'That which does not move after it is born?'
   'The egg.'
6. 'That which has no heart?'
   'A rock.'
7. 'Who is greater than the earth itself?'
   'A mother.'
8. 'Who is loftier than the heavens?'
   'The father.'
9. 'What is faster than the wind?'
   'The mind.'
10. 'More numerous than grass?'
    'Thoughts.'
11. 'How does one attain the highest virtue?'
    'Through liberality.'
12. 'How does one attain fame?'
    'Through gift.'
13. 'How does one attain happiness?'
    'Through good behaviour.'
14. 'How does one win appreciation?'
    'Through skill.'
15. 'What is the most valuable possession?'
    'Knowledge.'
16. 'The best gain of all?'
    'Health.'
17. 'The best among all kinds of happiness?'
    'Contentment.'

reputation. I came here with the purpose of meeting you, O virtuous king. I, therefore, grant you back the lives of all your brothers. You have won them back.'

And wonder of wonders, all the four Pandava brothers – Bheema, Arjuna, Nakula and Sahadeva – woke up as if from deep sleep.

They embraced each other and touched Yudhishthira's feet.

They were, I'm sure, quite ashamed to have been foolhardy and hasty in not listening to the *yaksha*.

Yudhishthira was born to Lord Yama, also called Dharmaraja, who keeps a log of the lives of people on earth. He is also the lord of justice. Since Yudhishthira was his son, he was also known as Dharmaputra. He was very fair and correct in his dealings. He always spoke the truth. So much so that, in the Kurukshetra war, when the false news of his son Ashwatthama's death was conveyed to Dronacharya, he insisted that it be corroborated by Yudhishthira. And Yudhishthira, in order to not lie, said, 'Ashwatthama, hathah, kunjarah' *(meaning 'an elephant named [this he murmurs] Ashwatthama is dead'). Upon hearing which Dronacharya dropped his weapons.*

THE WISE RAJA BHOJA AND THE THRONE OF VIKRAMADITYA

We all know the story of how the cowherds in a village stood on a mysterious mound and spoke very wisely. And how, underneath that mound, the king's men found the throne of the mighty, wise and wonderful king, Vikramaditya the Great.

Well, going forward, let us see what happened, shall we?

Raja Bhoja was utterly obsessed with the throne. Being a very wise and brave king himself, he felt that the throne of Vikramaditya would be perfect for him. So, he arranged for it to be placed in his court. He couldn't stop thinking about sitting on the magical throne, with its sixteen steps flanked by dolls on either side.

Well, one bright morning, the king had his royal bath with scented oils and perfumed scrubs, and then donned his royal robes. He went straight to the palace temple and prayed to the gods before going on to the royal durbar. He was as thrilled as a small child with a new toy. He was very anxious to sit on the wonderful throne, but he was not yet sure if the time was right.

After his whole day's work as king, that night when all was quiet, he went secretly into the beautiful throne room and put his foot respectfully on the first step.

A…nd…no sooner had he done that than an amazing thing happened!

There was a sound of tinkling laughter. The king stopped dead in his tracks. His raised his foot; he looked all around him in great surprise.

Whose voice was that?

There seemed to be no one around. He was alone. How very strange indeed!

'Who's that?' he thundered in his commanding voice. His voice echoed in the silence. How eerie!

The king shook his head. *I must be hearing things*, he told himself. He looked around once more.

And then, very cautiously, he put his foot again on the first step.

To his great surprise, the tinkling laughter rang out again. This time the king saw where it came from. He stood amazed. He could not believe his eyes. He could not trust his ears either.

The two dolls on either side of the first step were laughing at the king…and then one of them spoke.

'Dear Bhoja Raja, you are brave and wise. You are loved and respected by everyone. But do you know to whom this throne belongs? It belongs to the one and only – the great king Vikramaditya.'

'Yes, of course, I know that,' said the king.

The doll spoke again, 'O great king Bhoja, there has been no one like him either before or after. His glory was like the brilliant sun. In bravery he was like the lion. He spoke only the truth and was kind to his subjects. He had no equal as a warrior. Despite being such a great man, he was very humble.'

The king was silent.

The doll spoke again. 'To give you an example of his bravery and might, O king, I shall now tell you a story about him. Listen.'

The king sat down to listen to the story.
The doll began her tale…

'King Vikramaditya was fond of adventure. He was completely fearless. One day, a learned man came to him and said, "O king, you are a very brave man and like to achieve the impossible. What I am about to tell you might interest you."

'Indeed. Tell me,' said Vikramaditya.

"O king, just outside of your kingdom, Ujjaini, there is a holy river, a *pushkarini*. Across it lies a beautiful *swarna stambha* – a golden pillar. The wonder of it is that, as the sun moves up the sky, the *swarna stambha* also rises. At noon, my lord, as the sun touches the highest point in its path in the sky, the *stambha* touches the *surya mandala*, the sun."'

'And then?' asked Bhoja Raja, very curious.

'Well, Raja Vikramaditya was very excited. No sooner did he wake up in the morning than he set off in search of the holy river. What the learned man had said was true. There was a river exactly as he had described, and a *swarna stambha* lay across it. The fearless king Vikramaditya stepped on to the *stambha*, and do you know what happened? As the sun slowly glided up the sky, the *stambha* also rose.'

'And?' asked Bhoja Raja, feeling a little breathless.

'Well, as it rose upwards, it grew in height as well.'

Bhoja Raja was struck with great wonder.

'As the sun rose higher in the sky the *stambha* rose skywards. and as it moved higher and higher, the *stambha* too rose, growing ever taller. The king, sitting on it, began to get scorched by the heat. Exactly at noon the sun touched its zenith. And do you know what happened? *The golden pillar touched the* surya mandala.'

Bhoja Raja was amazed. He forgot to even breathe.

'The king was burnt almost black. He closed his eyes and folded his hands in prayer! He prayed to the sun god to save him, but he did not lose heart.'

The king had not moved. 'And then?' he said. His voice was a whisper.

The doll continued:

'Well, the sun god was well pleased with King Vikramaditya's fearlessness and courage. He blessed him and healed his burns.'

'I am indeed very pleased with you, O king, with your outstanding courage and bravery,' said the sun god. 'None other than you could have done that.' Surya blessed him with a long life and told him that he would shine with a new brilliance henceforth.

'Do you know what 'Vikramaditya' means? *Vikram* means courage and *aditya* means the sun. Therefore, *vikram* + *aditya* means one who is like the sun in his courage. Surya then presented Vikramaditya with a pair of dazzling divine earrings or '*karna kundala*s'. He told the king that they would always protect him and shower him with gold coins that could fill the river many times over, every day.'

Raja Bhoja sat perfectly still, listening with rapt attention. He had never heard anything like this in his whole life.

'As soon as the sun started to go down again towards the west, the *swarna stambha* gradually came down again. At sunset the divine pillar returned to its place across the river. Raja Vikramaditya got off and started back to his palace.'

Bhoja Raja was dumbfounded.

'There is more to this story,' said the doll.

'Oh,' said Bhoja Raja.

'On his way back, a man in need came to him and said, 'O king, O Vikramaditya, I have heard great praise of your kindness and large-heartedness. I am in the habit of feeding the poor every day, O king, but now I have no money. I request your highness to help me.'

'And do you know what Vikramaditya did? Without another thought, he handed over the hard-won *karna kundalas* to the man in need.'

Having completed the story, the doll asked Bhoja Raja, 'O king, now tell me this: have you ever heard of anyone as brave as King Vikramaditya? Or as kind and charitable? A person who had received the blessings of the sun god himself and yet gave away his divine gift to a stranger without a second thought?'

Raja Bhoja fell deep into thought. He knew he was neither as brave nor as generous as Vikramaditya.

The doll saw that the king was quiet. It asked, 'Do you think, O king, that you are fit to sit on his throne? A throne on which such a great and fearless king sat? If you can become as courageous and kind as he was, only then do you deserve to sit on this wonderful throne.' So saying, the doll fell silent.

The king could not fool himself. He returned to his chambers, but he could not sleep that night. He lay awake, tossing and turning, and wondered.

He made up his mind to become a stronger, kinder and a more just king. He started practising all these good qualities every day.

Every time he went back to climb up the next step, the two dolls at either end told him two more stories about Vikramaditya and his amazing qualities, and each time Raja Bhoja would step down to work hard at becoming a better man and a greater king.

Just imagine, there were sixteen steps going up to this magnificent throne, so this happened all of thirty-two times. And the dolls told him thirty-two stories in all.

At long last, Raja Bhoja felt that he was deserving enough to sit on the throne of Vikramaditya.

By this time, he had become a much better person – braver, kinder, humbler and stronger. He was not proud any more or selfish.

And by the time he could sit on the throne, he was a changed man and a wonderful king. But, sadly for him, he never got to sit on the throne of the great king Vikramaditya. And do you know why?

The time had come for the throne to go back to where it belonged. It belonged to Indra, the chief of the devas, who had given the throne to Vikramaditya as a gift. And no one else could use it.

Now, have we learnt something from this story? I'm sure we have.

We can all learn to be a little more brave, helpful, kind and unselfish, can we not?

The thirty-two dolls on Vikramaditya's throne were actually celestial nymphs. Indra, the chief of devas, pleased with Vikramaditya's righteousness, generosity, bravery and his upholding of the moral order as well as his amity with other kings, gifted him with this celestial throne. It had the magical power of enhancing the might and glory of King Vikramaditya to even greater heights.

HOW PRINCE RAMA SAVED KABANDHA, THE DEMON… BY ENDING HIS LIFE

Did I say that Mahabharata has countless stories that thrill? Well, the Ramayana, the other earlier epic, has no fewer.

The hero of the Ramayana is Rama, the Ikshvaku king of Ayodhya, and therefore called Ayodhyapati. Rama, his wife, Sita, and his brother, Lakshmana, spent fourteen years in exile – a period long enough for many adventures and encounters, and mishaps and misfortunes…

It was during this time that Sita was carried away by Ravana, the ten-headed king of Lanka. As Rama and Lakshmana scoured the forests, desperately looking for Sita, they were always alert and ready to face any enemy or danger that could waylay them.

One day, as the two were wandering in the woods near the ashram of Matanga Maharishi, they suddenly found themselves enveloped in a huge, dark cave. They walked into it quite fearlessly. In a while, they heard a loud roar.

Two large and hairy arms reached out, grabbing Rama in the right hand and Lakshmana in the left.

And they were hauled into what they now realized was – not a cave – but a MOUTH.

In a flash, Rama cut off the right arm and Lakshmana, the left. Looking up, they found themselves staring at a huge eye and an enormous set of teeth in the cavernous mouth in middle of a stomach.

Seeing this strange and frightening sight, Rama realized that this could not be anything but a rakshasa, and no ordinary one at that.

Appreciating the bravery of the young men, Kabandha, for that was the rakshasa's name, asked them whether they were indeed Rama and Lakshmana.

Upon hearing that they were Rama and Lakshmana, Kabandha bowed in reverence and said, 'O Rama, I'm blessed to have you come to me. I am Kabandha. I've waited all these years for you. If you will permit me, I shall tell you my story...'

The wounded Kabandha was now beginning to feel feeble.

'Of course, go ahead,' said the two princes. 'We mistook you for a cave and walked in – '

'My lord,' Kabandha continued, 'my story goes back to the time I was a *gandharva*, a celestial being and divine singer. My name was Vishwavasu. I prayed to Brahma and did penance for many years. At last Brahma appeared and granted me the boon of immortality.

'I became arrogant with my new-found invincibility and took my power for granted. I troubled everyone around me, earned the wrath of rishis by interrupting their yagnas...'

Kabandha paused to catch his breath, his energy was draining. He was dying...

Rama looked on kindly, waiting, knowing that Kabandha needed to speak. Kabandha went on, '... and then I turned on Indra, the supreme power of the devas and he used the *vajrayudha* on me in great anger…pushing my head into my torso.'

The *vajrayudha* was the strongest weapon ever. It was made of the indestructible, diamond-hard bones of the sage Dadhichi, who had sacrificed his life to help Indra win his battle with the demon Vritra. The *vajrayudha* was like a bolt of lightning that could annihilate even the most powerful enemy.

'Horrified and repentant, I pleaded that I had to feed myself somehow to survive. Indra, then, put a mouth in my belly and gave me extra-long arms to forage and feed myself.'

Once again Kabandha took a deep breath, gasping for air.

'Indra took pity on me finally and told me that I would regain my original form when Rama cut off my arms. I request you, O Rama, to please cremate me and send me on my way…'

And Rama followed his instructions and out of Kabandha's ashes rose the celestial, beautiful form of Vishwavasu, the *gandharva*, his palms together in humble gratitude to Rama.

As he departed to the heavens, the *gandharva* said, 'O Rama, you are the avatar of Lord Vishnu. You are indeed powerful and adept in the art of war and no one can defeat you. But remember that Ravana is extremely powerful and learned in all the sixty-four shastras. There is none in all the three worlds who does not fear him.

'So, beware. You will have to plan well to get the better of him. I would suggest you join hands with Sugreeva and help him get back his own kingdom from his brother Vali, who is now ruling the *vanara* kingdom of Kishkindha. Sugreeva is currently in exile in Rishyamukha mountain and lives in great fear of Vali. If you help him reclaim his power, his support will be key to help you defeat Ravana and thus rescue Sita.'

Vishwavasu also gave Rama directions to reach Rishyamukha mountain, saying, 'I wish you all success in your quest, Rama. May you be victorious.'

Thus, the horrifying giant with the gaping mouth in his belly and super-long arms regained his celestial form.

In paintings, artists have often shown Rama and Lakshmana sitting on Kabandha's arms, about to chop them off. Kabandha is shown with a gaping mouth on his stomach and one eye (sometimes, two), such as in depictions of him in temples. The detailed story of Kabandha is told in the third book, the Aranya Kanda, of the Ramayana.

NAHUSHA CHAKRAVARTI, THE KING WHO TURNED INTO A SERPENT

We shall now see what arrogance can do to even the strongest of people. It pays to have a sensible head on one's shoulders and not get carried away by one's achievements.

Don't believe that?

Well, the mighty king, Nahusha Chakravarti, got a taste of...well, not just a taste...but suffered prolonged misery because he got too big for his boots, so to say.

Nahusha was born to King Ayu of the Chandravanshi or Lunar Dynasty after much propitiation of the gods with prayers and yagnas.

King Ayu prayed to rishi Dattatreya and requested that an illustrious and invincible son, possessed of great qualities, be born to him, someone who would be a fitting heir to the throne. Soon after,

Ayu's queen, Prabha, gave birth to a healthy and handsome son.

Meanwhile, at about the same time, possibly on a whim, the goddess Parvati requested Shiva to take her to the most beautiful garden in the whole world. Shiva took her to the celestial garden of Nandana Vana. In that garden grew the Kalpavriksha, a tree which had emerged from the Samudra Manthan, the churning of the Ocean of Milk by the devas and the asuras.

The magical Kalpavriksha had the quality of granting any wish asked of it. And Parvati knew that, of course.

Instantly, she wished for a daughter.

And lo and behold, a lovely, magical maiden emerged from the Kalpavriksha. Parvati named her Ashokasundari. She wished also for a perfect husband for her – and that would be the great emperor Nahusha.

In the course of time, Ashokasundari married Nahusha. One amazing thing was that Ashokasundari was born long before Nahusha and had been born a full-fledged maiden. So, she waited patiently for Nahusha to be born and ask for her hand, which he did. (There is yet another interesting story here which, for convenience's sake, I have shortened.)

Nahusha was tutored by the great sage Vashishtha and proved an able pupil. He grew up to be brave and fearless, a skilled warrior of renown, who helped his father expand his kingdom.

Upon King Ayu's death, Nahusha took over the reins of the empire. He ruled his kingdom righteously and ably. He was wise, kind and took the right decisions. It was no wonder that he was loved by the people of his empire.

At such a time of supremacy for Nahusha, Indra, the chief of the devas, had to go into hiding for some time for a wrongdoing of his.

The devas invited Nahusha Chakravarti, being the brilliant and righteous king that he was, to be their next Indra, their chief. And he was appointed the officiating Indra. He now lived in Swarga Loka.

Well, what more could he want? He did not realize, though, that this was the beginning of his downfall.

As he grew in power and pelf, Nahusha's humility plummeted. The fact that he was now Indra, went to his head. He started disdaining the moral code. He could brook no criticism and turned a deaf ear to the advice of the learned. He treated respected sages like vassals. They had to do his bidding. He lagged in his service to the devas. All his accumulated good karma from kind deeds diminished and finally dwindled into nothing.

However, he was too full of his ego to notice the downward slide his life was taking... As we all know, with power comes pride. But then pride comes before a fall and that's what happened with Nahusha too!

His arrogance now knew no bounds and he became greedy as well.

He now aspired to marry the beautiful Indrani, Indra's wife. But did Indrani want to marry him? No, of course not. She was too fond of her husband, Indra, who was in hiding.

Nahusha started pestering her and this upset Indrani a lot. She went to Brihaspati, the guru and mentor of the devas, for guidance. 'O respected guru Brihaspati,' she said, 'I need your advice. Nahusha, the new chief of the devas, wants me to become his wife.'

'Uh-oh,' sighed Brihaspati, 'That is not right at all. You are Indra's wife...'

'And I love my husband dearly, O rishi. I will not think of another in his place.'

'Have you told him that?' asked Brihaspati.

'Indeed, I have,' cried Indrani, 'but he will not listen. He is after me to accept him. What shall I do, O respected father?'

'Well, we will have to teach him a lesson in our own way,' said the wise Brihaspati, smiling sardonically. 'Don't lose heart, O daughter! We'll need to use a clever trick here. His arrogance is leading him to his downfall, anyway… He is but hastening the arrival of his bad days, and very soon, by this improper behaviour.'

Sage Brihaspati's face was grim as he continued, 'However, you'll have to employ some trickery…'

'I'll do as you tell me, O wise one,' said Indrani, desperate but determined.

'Good. Then do exactly as I say. Don't reveal to him your dislike of him. Pretend to play along. He will readily fall for it.'

'I will, O sage,' said Indrani. 'Bless me so that I may succeed in teaching him a lesson…'

'My child, you have my blessings,' the sage replied, 'but plan your strategy well. Tell him to come to you… the rest I shall leave to your intelligence.'

And so Indrani went back to her palace and pondered over how to handle Nahusha. She was very wise and intelligent, and had often guided her husband, Indra, on matters of vital importance.

She didn't lack for a scheme now. Her face lit up as she hit upon just the perfect ploy to make the overreaching Nahusha mend his ways.

She sent word to Nahusha that she was indeed eager to meet him and that he should come to her palace.

And not just that. Her message said, 'Please come in a vehicle befitting your royal status, your highness.'

Nahusha was overjoyed. 'As you wish, O queen,' he responded. 'I shall come over in an ornate coach drawn by my best horses.'

'Oh no, no,' said the queen. 'That would not do justice to your Indra *padavi* now, O king. You should do better than that.'

'Oh, I must, of course,' agreed the king readily, playing right into her hands. 'Not only are you beautiful, Indrani, but also very perceptive. Please suggest a better mode of travel.'

Indrani, the smart queen that she was, did not let the opportunity go. 'O king, you should arrive in an opulent palanquin. And it should be borne by seven illustrious sages – the Saptarishis, no less.'

'Indeed,' gloated Nahusha gleefully, immodesty clouding his thinking. 'Who better than the Saptarishis? They had better make themselves useful. It will be an honour for them to carry Nahusha's palanquin.'

And so it happened that he set out in a palanquin, dressed in silks and gems befitting his status, carried by the seven eminent sages.

These were the most revered of the sages of the time. They were men of intellectual brilliance and meditative powers. The sages felt dishonoured and insulted by Nahusha's behaviour. But his Indra *padavi* had to be respected.

Carrying the palanquin was a difficult task for them. They were not used to doing the work of palanquin bearers. They suffered and sweated as they walked the distance to Indrani's palace. Nahusha, on the other hand, was in a great hurry to reach Indrani's palace. He kept urging the sages to walk faster and faster.

Six of the rishis, who were taller, were able to walk fast enough, but the shortest was, as we all know – Agastya. Agastya Maharishi was very powerful among the rishis. He was highly learned in grammar and was the author of many medical texts. His physical prowess too was daunting. But he was very short and his strides were small. The palanquin dipped on his side. He almost had to run to keep up with the others. Now, no one who had any inkling of his greatness would demean him, but Nahusha, in his proud, haughty state of mind, could not stop himself from taunting Agastya.

At one point, he got so impatient that he put out his foot and prodded the great sage on the shoulder saying, '*Kumbhadimba, sarpa, sarpa*,' which meant, 'you, born of a pot, go faster, faster!'

Agastya, who already felt exhausted and humiliated, felt his wrath flow over. He turned and cursed the king, '*Sarpo bhava*! (Be you a serpent!)'

And lo and behold! Nahusha slithered out of the palanquin, transformed into a huge serpent and fell to earth… Realizing his folly, Nahusha fell at the great sage Agastya's feet and begged his pardon.

'O sage, please forgive me my audacity, my disrespect of you,' he said, now humbled. 'My pride blinded me.'

Agastya would not relent. 'What has been done is done, Nahusha. You have intelligence enough to distinguish between right and wrong. Henceforth, you can remain in this state and repent.'

Nahusha begged, 'Please, O mighty sage, I'm prepared to do my penance. But I beg of you to redeem me. O kindly sage, do not condemn me to be a serpent forever.'

Finally, Sage Agastya took pity on Nahusha. 'Well, there is redemption for you,' he granted, 'but it will be a long time coming.'

And then the sage went on... 'In the Dwapara Yuga, during Mahabharata, the Pandavas will be in exile in the forests. And at that time, it will so happen that you will get Bheema into your stronghold and not let go...you will, at that time, sap him of his strength and regain yours.

'Yudhishthira, the all-knowing one, your own descendant in thousands of years, upon seeing his dear brother in distress, will entreat you to release him.

'You can then ask him questions of moral importance and the most significant truths. And he will answer with great wisdom. At that point you will be redeemed and regain your human form.'

Thereafter, Nahusha roamed the forests as a huge serpent. But he was deeply repentant. He realized how badly he had fallen from grace. Yet, being a snake, he committed the wrongs that a snake would do. Hundreds and hundreds of years passed.

The Kaurava brothers defeated their Pandava cousins in a game of *chaturanga*. The Pandavas paid the price by losing their kingdom. They had to go on a fourteen-year exile into the forests, giving up all the luxuries of a royal life.

During that time, while camping in a forest of great calm and beauty, Bheema took off on a hunt. He was chasing his quarry, when all of a sudden, he was taken aback by what he saw! There right in front of him, poised to strike and tangle him in its massive coils, was an ominous, ferocious, gigantic serpent. It was much larger than any he had ever seen. In the blink of an eye, the serpent wrapped itself around the great Bheema and started to squeeze the life-breath out of him.

Bheema, who had the strength of 16,000 elephants and the ferocity of a tiger, for the first time in his life, felt frail and helpless. He felt all his energy drain away! Much as he tried, he could not extricate himself from the huge serpent's stranglehold. He begged and pleaded with the serpent to let him go.

The serpent told him that he had waited for this moment for thousands of years. He told Bheema of his life as Nahusha Chakravarti and how he was compelled by fate to devour Bheema. Meanwhile, Yudhishthira came looking for his brother. He was astounded to see his all-powerful brother, upon whom they all relied for protection, completely helpless in the coils of an enormous serpent.

Yudhishthira too begged the serpent to release Bheema. He promised that he would get fitting food for him.

Nahusha, the serpent, only hissed menacingly, 'If you have any sense, save yourself, O Yudhishthira, or you will become my next meal.'

'I beg of you to free my brother,' beseeched Yudhishthira. 'Ask of me anything in return.'

'Well,' said Nahusha, 'I had been told by the great sage Agastya that you of the wise intellect and humble demeanour will answer questions that I ask and thus relieve me of this curse that I've suffered for centuries! I am Nahusha the illustrious king, who through my foolhardiness and arrogance came to be cursed to live the life of a serpent.'

'Yes, of course,' Yudhishthira agreed instantly, 'ask whatever you want to. I shall answer to the best of my ability.'

And so it came to pass that Nahusha asked Yudhishthira questions of great import and Yudhishthira answered him wisely and knowledgeably.

Nahusha, satisfied at long last with the answers to his queries, uncoiled himself and released Bheema. And quite astonishingly, he gradually regained his original form of Nahusha and with that his virtuous disposition too.

He had learned his lesson the hard way. And what a punishment it had been!

In the fourteenth year of their exile, the Pandavas were in agyatavasa *or living incognito. They had taken refuge with King Virata in the Matsya kingdom. The story of Nahusha, his fall from grace and the travails of Indrani and Indra were recounted to Yudhishthira and Draupadi by their uncle Shalya to afford them solace in their own sufferings.*

MAHABALI CHAKRAVARTI, THE KING WHO WAS TOO RIGHTEOUS FOR HIS OWN GOOD

From one great king, we come to another. Not because they were similar in their disposition, but because each of them was almost superhuman in his achievements as a king…and therefore gained the title of 'Chakravarti'.

This is a story of a king who was a *daitya*, a demon by birth. But what a righteous and wonderful king he was! We are talking here of Mahabali Chakravarti, who was the grandson of Prahlada, the great devotee of Lord Vishnu, who in turn was the son of the rakshasa king Hiranyakashipu.

So that makes Mahabali the great-grandson of Hiranyakashipu!

You see, it takes all kinds to make a family tree. Thankfully, Mahabali did not inherit the qualities of his great-grandfather. He was pious, right-thinking and compassionate, and was much loved by the people of his kingdom. He was also a devotee of Vishnu. You could say he was more in the mould of his grandfather Prahlada.

Still, he was an ambitious king all right. He belonged to the netherworld, the Patala Loka. But then, he also conquered the earth, Bhu Loka, and the heavens, the Indra Loka. An illustrious king, who rose through his exemplary behaviour to a level beyond every other king, was deemed fit for the position of Indra. Mahabali was in line for the next Indra *padavi*. Such was his might and power.

Well, would Indra happily hand over the reins of his kingdom to another? Obviously not.

So, where would Indra go but to Lord Vishnu for help, for the latter was sure to support him? And, as we already know, Mahabali himself was an ardent devotee of Lord Vishnu.

'Vishnu, my lord,' said Indra, 'Mahabali is a great king, no doubt, but it is not right that he should take away my kingdom and I say nothing. He is my cousin, and I don't want to go to battle with him. In any case, he is too powerful now for me to take on. I need your help, O lord. I don't want to lose my kingdom.'

'Well,' Vishnu replied wisely, 'Mahabali has rightfully conquered the devas and gained control of Indra Loka, remember that... and he is a righteous king too. Having said that, I can understand your problem, Indra, for you cannot be without a kingdom either.'

This was a sticky situation for Lord Vishnu. He could understand Indra's anxiety, but he could not deny Mahabali his rightly won dominions. He was a ruler par excellence. His kingdom was peaceful and prosperous, and the people were very happy.

And Vishnu's kindliness towards his devotees was unsurpassed.

Now, he was torn between solving Indra's dilemma and being just to Mahabali. He had to keep both his devotees happy, you see.

So he mulled it over and decided to wait for the right opportunity to arise. Vishnu was an expert at getting what he wanted, if not in a straightforward way, then through clever tactics. He also felt that, much as he wanted to not displease Mahabali, Indra's demand for his kingdom was not totally without reason.

He waited for the right time to find a solution.

That moment came soon enough. As all powerful emperors of the time did, Mahabali announced that he was undertaking the performance of the Ashwamedha Yagna. During the yagna, as per tradition, he also announced that he would give away in charity anything that was asked of him.

Well, now things were made easy for Vishnu.

The day of the yagna arrived. The list of guests was longer than ever seen in any Ashwamedha Yagna. There were devas. And *daitya*s. And all the kings on earth.

The grand spectacle was breathtaking!

When the *daana* (the process of charity) began, the queue was unending. And Mahabali kept his word. Whatever the request was, it was granted to each person. Cattle, grain, gold, silver, jewels, silks, land, money...there was no end to the king's largesse.

Thc qucuc was almost ovcr...

But at the very end of it waited a small Brahmin boy. The king was a little surprised. What could this child want?

He knelt in front of the boy and, with folded hands, asked him to name his request. Charity was to be offered humbly and not with a show of might.

'What is it that you wish, my boy?' asked the king.

And the boy smiled mysteriously and said, 'Oh, I just want the amount of land that can be measured by three steps of mine.'

'Indeed. Only that much?' asked the king. 'Are you sure you don't want anything more? A village? A few villages? Cattle...or jewels?'

The king's counsellor and guru, the sage Sukracharya, was standing by his side. He sensed there was more to this little boy than met the eye. 'My lord, it would pay to be cautious,' he warned the king. 'I sense a trick in the boy's request.'

The king turned to him and said, smiling, 'Today is a day to grant any wish asked of me and I should not go back on my word. Let him ask for whatever he wants. I shall give it.'

The king turned back to the boy and said, 'Go ahead, ask of me anything you wish.'

'I need only three measures of land the size of my feet,' repeated the lad.

'Then so be it,' said the king.

No sooner had he said that than the most unbelievable thing happened. The small boy grew bigger and bigger, until he reached a gigantic size, slowly revealing himself to be none other than Lord Vishnu… in the form of 'Trivikrama'. *Tri* means *three* and *vikrama* means *stride*. Trivikrama, also known as Vamana, took back the three worlds by measuring them with his three steps.

He planted one foot on the earth and with it measured all of Mahabali's kingdom in Bhu Loka… all of the earth. The other foot he raised to the skies and measured all of Indra Loka…all of the heavens.

And then he looked at Mahabali with an enigmatic smile and asked, 'Where now, O king, is the land for my third step?'

Mahabali knew then that his lord and master, Vishnu, had presented himself. He was filled with humility. He knelt down in devotion and bowed his head, saying, 'I offer you my head, my lord, for I have nothing else.'

And so, Vishnu, the Trivikrama, put his foot gently on his devotee Mahabali's head and conveyed him to the netherworld, Patala Loka.

It is said that Mahabali Chakravarti still rules in Patala Loka.

During the churning of the Ocean of Milk or Samudra Manthan to obtain amrit, *one end of Vasuki (the snake who consented to be used as the rope) was held by the devas and the other end by the* daityas.

Now it so happened that the chief of the daityas *was none other than the great King Mahabali. It was he who led the churn from their side. At a later juncture he got to have some of the* amrit *that made him immortal or* chiranjeevi. *At the Onam festival of Kerala and the Kartikai festival of Tamil Nadu, Mahabali, who is believed to reside in Patala Loka, is welcomed by his devotees to visit the earth. Lamps are lit in his welcome and home-fronts are bedecked with beautiful flower decorations and rangoli or* kolam.

VIDYOTTAMA, THE PRINCESS WHO TRANSFORMED A COWHERD INTO A GREAT POET

A very, very long time ago, in the city of Ujjaini, ruled the famous king, Vikramaditya. He was a man of legendary valour, wisdom and power. His kingdom extended from the Indus Valley in the west to Bengal in the east, and from the Himalayas in the north to the Narmada in the south.

He was an exceptionally brave and generous king, and his subjects were happy and content under his rule. There are many, many thrilling stories about him, but this one is not about him but rather his equally exceptional daughter – princess Vidyottama.

She was named Gunamanjari at birth by her parents. Under her tutor, Rajguru Vararuchi, she learned to excel in the Shastras and the Vedas. She was also proficient in the use of weapons and the art of warfare.

And, of course, she was very well aware of her accomplishments, and with them her pride grew as well. As she grew older, she became more intelligent and beautiful with every passing day. When the time came for her to choose a suitor for herself, she found no one to equal her. There was none that could match her in wit, intelligence, erudition and her ability to hold her own on important topics. And could she have married someone who could not better her?

No, of course not.

So she announced that she would marry the one person who could beat her at *shastrartha* (debate on the scriptures) and prove that he was more intelligent and learned than her.

Princes and scholars from all over the country flocked to Ujjaini to take up her challenge. They all boasted of great education and eloquence in arguments and discussions.

But not one of them could beat her.

What could she do? They all had to be sent away. And some of those scholars were furious!

'She is too headstrong,' declared one. 'So what if she is so intelligent and learned? We are no less.'

'Yes,' agreed another bright spark, who had been rejected. 'Not only is she proud of her learning, she is also very haughty about her beauty… '

'It is time she learnt a lesson,' said another spitefully.

'Well, what are we waiting for?' said the first. 'Let's teach her a lesson she will not forget in a hurry.'

'We will make her regret that she did not marry any of us,' said the third. 'That should serve her right.' They vowed to marry her off to the greatest fool and imbecile they could lay their hands on.

The search began.

The group of scholars got together and travelled the length and breadth of the country, going from village to village. But they could find no one foolish enough to meet their requirement.

At last weary of travelling, they came to a small hamlet. Passing beneath a tree, they looked up to find a young man upon it. He was sawing away at a heavy branch.

Nothing really unusual about that.

What was remarkable was that he was seated on the side of the branch that would come down, when cut. He was sure to fall and break his neck, but he seemed blissfully unaware of this danger.

'Hey, look at that, my friends,' said one of the scholars in puzzlement, 'do you see what I see?'

'Oh God,' said the second, 'he is cutting the branch from under him.'

'Oh no,' said the third, 'I have not seen a greater fool in my life.'

They laughed until their stomachs ached.

'Are you thinking what I am thinking?' asked the first, wiping the tears of laughter streaming from his eyes. He had a habit of speaking in riddles.

'Yes, indeed,' the other two nodded. They had found the very person they wanted. They were delighted that they had found the ideal candidate for the princess's hand. They coaxed and cajoled him to come down from his perch.

'Hey, you,' said the first, very tickled, 'O maharaja of fools. Please climb down.'

'Yes. We have great plans for you,' mocked the second.

'Why should you be doing such a mean job when you are fit for a princess?' demanded the third, hiding a smile.

They threatened to kill him if he didn't do exactly as told. The young man had no option but to give in.

They gave him detailed instructions and dressed him up in fine clothes. They sent word to the princess that they had found an excellent scholar who wanted to accept her challenge. The princess was overjoyed that she was going to meet her match at last.

Afraid that if the foolish young man opened his mouth, he would reveal himself to be the fool that he was, the scholars gave him strict orders to keep quiet. He was to speak only in gestures when the princess asked questions.

They also told the princess that, being a man of very high intellect, this great young man spoke only in gestures! The princess was very impressed indeed.

The day of the *shastrartha* arrived. The princess sat opposite the young man, who was dressed in silks and brocade. The princess raised a finger. She meant to say that Brahman is one and that there is only one universal truth.

The young man, who was trembling with fear, thought that the princess was threatening to poke him in the eye.

He immediately raised two fingers, meaning that if she poked him in one eye, he would poke her in both her eyes.

The scholars interpreted that he was telling her that God is one, but the Atman and Brahman are two.

Much encouraged by his erudition, she next showed her palm denoting the five senses. The young man thought she was going to slap him.

He extended his closed fist, meaning he might punch her if she dared to do so.

The scholars quickly intervened and told the princess that since she had indicated the five senses, he had revealed the control of the senses by closing his fist. The princess was delighted indeed to see that she had met more than her match in intelligence.

So coached cleverly by the wicked scholars, the foolish young man won the challenge using mere gestures alone!

The princess and the young man were married with great pomp and splendour befitting her royal birth. But she soon discovered that the young man was a great fool. She had been deceived. She was very upset. That evening, she got the whole story out of him at the point of a sword. But she was a very intelligent young woman and decided upon a plan to make him fit to be her husband.

'Listen carefully,' she said, pointing the sword at the terrified young man.

'There is a temple to the goddess Kali in the palace garden. Go there this evening. At the exact hour of twilight, the goddess will step out for her walk. Watch carefully. As soon as she comes out, go and shut yourself in. Bolt the door from within.'

The young man was trembling with fright. He begged the princess's pardon and pleaded with her to let him go.

'No,' said the princess, 'you are my husband now. I shall have to make you worthy of me.'

The young man had no choice but to obey her instructions.

The princess went on, 'When the goddess returns and sees the door closed, she will knock at it. Do *not* open it. She will get very angry. She is the goddess Kali, the fearsome one. She will threaten you, but do not give in. Do not, *under any condition,* open the door.'

The young man quaked with fear. But did he dare disobey the princess?

Of course not.

'Finally, seeing your determination,' the princess went on, 'she will ask you what you want. Ask her to write the all-powerful "*beejakshara*" on your tongue with her hand.'

The young man was trembling like a leaf. He wished with all his heart that the princess would let him go.

'She will agree,' said the princess, 'and ask you to open the door so that she may do so. Do not fall for the trick. Tell her that you will put your tongue out through the keyhole so that she may write the *beejakshara* on it.'

Isn't the seed what all plants grow from? In the same way, all learning has come from the *beejakshara*. The *seed word.*

And do you know what the *beejakshara* is?

The Sanskrit letter 'Om'.

Well, since the young man was petrified and also too foolish to ask questions, he did exactly as he was told.

That evening, as darkness set in, he went to the temple in the palace garden and locked himself in just when the goddess set out for her evening stroll. When she returned, she found the door shut.

When she knocked on the door, the foolish young man refused to open the door. The goddess flew into a rage and threatened him. She coaxed and cajoled, but the young man refused to let her in.

At last, realizing that he was very determined, she conceded, 'All right, tell me what you want?'

'O goddess,' he said, 'you will have to write the *beejakshara* on my tongue.'

'So be it,' said the goddess. 'Open the door so that I may do so.'

'No, I shall put my tongue out through the keyhole and you may write the *beejakshara* on it,' said the young man.

And so the goddess, Kali, wrote the *beejakshara* on his tongue with her divine fingers.

And then, do you know, the most amazing and wonderful thing happened!

No sooner had the goddess written the *beejakshara* on his tongue than the foolish young man was transformed into a wonderfully learned one. In that instant he turned into a great scholar and poet.

All knowledge came to him in the blink of an eye. Words flowed off his tongue like a stream.

He opened the door and prostrated himself at the goddess's feet. He thanked her over and over again. Through the goddess's grace, he had become a wonderful poet. What more could he ask for?

With tears of joy he recited his very first sloka in praise of goddess Kali, called the '*Shyamala Dandakam*' (Shyamala being yet another name for Kali). The goddess blessed him and said that henceforth he would be called Kalidasa, a 'slave to the goddess Kali'. He had no equal in poetry and in the beauty of words.

Kalidasa, overcome with gratitude and joy, went straight to the palace. The princess was waiting with bated breath. She saw the radiance of knowledge and enlightenment on the young man's face and knew that he was a changed person. She was overjoyed.

Then she put a question to him...a very famous one – and a rather difficult one. In the ancient language of Sanskrit, she asked him, '*Asthi kaschith vaagarthaha*? (Is there any meaning to your words?)'

Kalidasa gazed at the princess in awe and said, 'From now on, you are my guru. You showed me the path to knowledge.'

And Kalidasa, who was no longer a foolish young man, wrote three beautiful poetical stories. They were called the *kavyas*. The first word of each of them began with the three words the princess spoke.

The *kavya* named *Kumarasambhava* ('the birth of the lord Kumara') began with the word *asthi.*

The first word of the *kavya Meghaduta* ('the cloud messenger') was *kaschith*.

And the next one titled *Raghuvamsa* ('the Raghu dynasty') started with the word *vaak*.

Such was his mastery of words.

And that was how the greatest poet of India was born!

Do you know that Kalidasa, the great poet, was one of the 'navaratna' *or 'nine gems' of the famous king Maharaja Vikramaditya's court? Yes, the very same Vikramaditya who climbed the* swarna sthamba *and won the magical* karna kundalas *from the sun god.*

It is said that this prolific poet spent most of his life in Ujjaini and was a great favourite of Raja Vikramaditya. He was known for the beauty of his language and the art of creating wonderful 'upama' *or similes.*

RUKMINI, THE COURAGEOUS PRINCESS

You do know by now that Krishna was the ruler of Dwarka. As Dwarka *adhipati*, the king, he had many queens.

Here we shall be talking about the queen who was the favourite of Lord Krishna. She was beautiful beyond compare and bold, and had many more wonderful qualities. Rukmini was the daughter of the king of Vidarbha and the sister of Rukmi.

When the time came for her to get married, the king set up a *swayamvara* for her, as was the custom in those days for princesses, where she could choose her own husband from among the suitors present.

On an invitation from the king, eligible young rulers and princes of other kingdoms, young men of fame and fortune, of great valour and good looks would arrive and vie for the princess's hand. The aspirants would fall over each other to prove themselves fit for the princess.

Often there would be a daunting challenge or competition to be won. In this way, only the best among equals would be chosen.

Now here was a problem. Rukmini's brother, Rukmi, wanted her to marry Shishupala, his dear friend and the ruler of Chedi.

We have read about him in our very first story in this book.

Well, he was a great ruler and a skilled warrior as well but not a very nice person. He was arrogant and ill-mannered. And he was, as we know, a sworn enemy of Krishna.

A knotty issue if ever there was one!

The princess Rukmini had heard great stories of Krishna and had lost her heart to him. She had heard of his heroism and victories against daunting enemies such as Jarasandha. She wanted to marry him and him alone.

It so happened that princess Rukmini's father, the king himself, wanted her to marry the charming and powerful king of Dwarka, Krishna, but her brother was adamant and had set his face against this suit.

'But I love Krishna, Rukmi,' cried the lovely young Rukmini, 'and I will marry him, not Shishupala.'

'That you shall not, if I have any say in the matter,' roared her brother. 'You shall marry Shishupala, and no other.'

He cleverly convinced his father that his sister should be married off to his friend.

'Listen now, sister dear, to me –
None other than Shishupala will you marry.
This moment shall I tell our father...
Not an instant shall I tarry.'

'I shall not, I shall not, I shall not,' wept the spirited young princess, 'and you cannot make me.' She stamped her foot in anger. She was very determined.

But, finally, Rukmi got his way.

An engagement was arranged between Shishupala and the princess Rukmini. As the day of the marriage approached, Rukmini grew more and more restless. Her brother kept a very close watch on her and would not let her go anywhere without an escort. She felt trapped, like a caged bird.

But then, not for nothing was Rukmini a strong-willed princess. She knew that if she kept quiet, she would be married off to Shishupala, whom she did not like one bit. 'I would hate that,' she told herself. 'I have to do something before it is too late.'

She sat and thought carefully for quite a while until she hit upon the very plan. She knew exactly what she was going to do.

Rukmini called one of her girls-in-waiting and whispered in her ear, 'Fetch my palm leaf and writing reed. Go on, hurry.'

'What's on your mind, my princess?' asked the girl, curious and worried for her mistress.

'Don't you start asking me questions now,' chided Rukmini.

The girl rushed away and was back in no time with what her lady had asked for.

In the next few minutes, the determined Rukmini had written a letter to Krishna. She asked him to rescue her from her marriage to Shishupala: 'You must come, O Krishna. I will marry nonc but you. And if you don't arrive on time, this life will not be worth living.'

She beckoned her girl-in-waiting once more. 'Hmm… now let me see who can be trusted with this letter,' she mused.

…And she knew.

'Of course – Sunanda, my friend! He is the only one who can be trusted. Oh, thank the gods! Now run along and hand this over to him. Tell him to hurry.'

Very soon Sunanda handed over Rukmini's letter to Krishna.

But… did this story have a happy ending?

Yes.

Krishna did not waste a moment. He did come to fetch Rukmini – before her brother could force her into marrying Shishupala. As he carried Rukmini away with him, her brother, Rukmi, put up a huge fight. There was a roaring battle between the two, but Krishna defeated Rukmi and won the beautiful Rukmini for his wife.

This is how the gutsy Rukmini stood her ground and married Lord Krishna, the person she wanted to marry. Rukmini was considered the avatar or reincarnation of Lakshmi, the consort of Lord Vishnu himself, in her previous birth. And, of course, Krishna was the reincarnation of Vishnu.

In those days, princesses often drew their names from their father's name or kingdom. Rukmini was also called Vaidarbhi as she belonged to Vidarbha, and Bhaishmaki, because she was King Bhishma's daughter. She had four brothers and Rukmi was the eldest of them.

SHIBI CHAKRAVARTI, THE KING WHO WAS ASTONISHINGLY CHARITABLE

There are stories upon stories of great valour, bravery and sacrifice in our Puranas and scriptures, and in the great epics – the Mahabharata and the Ramayana.

There are tales of extreme greed, jealousy and betrayal too. Both of these make for dramatic accounts. But when men and women – and in our stories here, kings and queens – rise above their anger, petty jealousies and greed, and show outstanding compassion and love and sacrifice or bravery and courage, it makes for a fascinating read.

Such, one would say, is the power of good. And we do need plenty of it in our world today.

Without making you hold your breath for too long, let me introduce you to yet another exceptional king.

Shibi or Shivi Chakravarti, as he was called, was a Chandravanshi – a descendant of the kings of the

Lunar Dynasty. He was an illustrious ruler – kind, extremely charitable and wise – who very capably ruled over a sprawling kingdom.

The title of Chakravarti was adopted in those days by very powerful kings of huge empires, who were acknowledged by the kings of smaller surrounding kingdoms as their superior. They attained the title of 'Chakravarti' by performing the Rajasuya Yagna or the Ashwamedha Yagna, to which they invited all the other kings of the land.

However, our king Shibi was famed for more than just that. His reputation of being the most compassionate and just ruler had spread far and wide. He was the supreme ruler of all three worlds – Deva Loka, Bhu Loka and Patala Loka.

It was said that anyone who came to him for help would never leave empty-handed. And just how benevolent was he? I mean, there must be quite a few kind and helpful people around us, isn't it? When we need help, we think of them first, because they jump at any chance to help.

Yes, yes, I agree such people are rare, but they are there all right. And they do make the world go round.

Shibi, we can say, was one of those rulers whose charity was boundless. He considered it his bounden duty to protect the weak and helpless...be it the people of his kingdom or the animals, birds and even plants and trees.

In a sense, he was a sage king, considerate and understanding.

Well, time went by…

He won the love of all his subjects and the respect of his ministers and courtiers – and, of course, the benediction of the sages. There was much talk about his exemplary qualities among even the devas.

Indra, the chief of the devas, as we know, always felt his Indra *padavi*, or supreme position, was under threat from these superhuman kings! He became very curious to find out whether all these tall claims about Raja Shibi were true. So he and his friend, Agni, hatched a plan.

One sunny day, when Raja Shibi was holding court as usual in his palace, surrounded by sprawling gardens, a very unexpected thing happened. A beautiful dove, pursued by a fierce falcon, flew into the court in terror and fell trembling on the Raja's lap.

'O kind Rrrr…aja Shibi – please, oh please, save me from the falcon,' cried the dove tremulously. 'It is bent on killing me.'

The king immediately placed a caring hand over the dove and said in a kindly voice, 'Do not fear, O dove. You are under my protection now. I'll make sure that the falcon does not hurt you.'

The falcon that had come chasing the dove, spoke, 'The dove is my meal, O king. You cannot deprive me of my food. I'm starving.'

The king turned to the falcon and said in a firm voice, 'The dove has taken refuge with me. There is no way that I'm going to hand it over to you. I'm duty-bound to protect the life of whoever takes shelter with me.'

'What of *me*?' demanded the angry falcon. 'What about *my* life? The dove is my food. I'll die of hunger. What about your compassion for *me*? Isn't it your duty to save *me* too?'

The king was in a quandary. If he saved the dove from the falcon, he was being unjust to the falcon; and if he let the falcon kill the dove, he was being cruel to the dove.

Being the compassionate and just king he was, Shibi wanted to be fair to both the dove and the falcon. A very difficult task indeed. He decided he could not sacrifice the dove's life to save the falcon's. But he could not deprive the falcon of its meal either.

The king thought deeply for a while. Then he spoke firmly, 'Ask of me any other food in the dove's place. I'll willingly give you whatever you ask for.'

The falcon looked at him and said, 'So be it, O king. What is it you can offer me in place of the dove?'

The king offered all kinds of delicious meat from the royal kitchens. But the falcon refused them all. And then it looked at the king and said, 'How about you, O king? How about your flesh? The flesh of a king of such valour, compassion, generosity and wisdom, should indeed be delectable.'

The king did not waste a moment.

'Bring out the royal scales, my *tula bharam*,' he commanded. 'I want my flesh to be weighed on the scales to equal the dove's weight.'

The courtiers looked on in amazement.

'The king is offering his flesh to the falcon…' they whispered to each other in utter horror.

'His compassion is going to cost him dearly,' lamented one.

'A small token of flesh should do, to equal the dove...I suppose,' said a third, sighing heavily.

The whole court was watching the scene, stunned.

The dove was placed on one side on the weighing scale. The king cut off flesh from his right thigh and put it on the other side.

The dove weighed more.

The king cut off more flesh and put it on the weighing scale.

And the dove continued to weigh more...

The king cut off his limb and placed it on the scale. The weighing scale tipped on the side of the dove again.

By now, the wise king knew that something unusual was at work here.

But he had given his word to the falcon, and he would keep it, he resolved.

The king cut off his other lower limb too and had it placed on the scale...

The dove weighed more, yet again.

Seeing this, the king told his attendants to help him on to the measure.

The weighing scale instantly came on a level with the dove.

The courtiers were in tears. But the king was

unperturbed. His head was bowed in prayer, his eyes were closed.

He had offered himself in place of the dove.

And that instant, a miracle happened.

The falcon and the dove transformed into the gods Indra and Agni.

They had planned to test the truth of Raja Shibi's glory and fame.

It was indeed true. His compassion and honour were without blemish. He was truly a great man and a virtuous king. Indra and Agni blessed Shibi and heaped praises on him.

He regained his full body and shone with new splendour.

And then, of course, he ruled for many, many more years over his vast dominions, winning more glory.

Shibi Chakravarti was supposed to have conquered the entire world and performed the Ashwamedha Yajna. He was famed for his charitable nature. He never refused anything asked of him. It is said that he had once sacrificed his own son to satisfy Brahma. Astonished at the king's incredible magnanimity, Brahma restored the king's son to life.

ACKNOWLEDGEMENTS

In this journey of reliving the stories, I have not been alone.

I have had some very young friends read them and give a jubilant thumbs up to the tales...

My family has afforded me both feedback and help whenever I was struggling with tech-related hiccups, and coughed and sputtered like a rusted engine.

Vatsala of Hachette India has been kind and helpful, and dealt with the stories with a gentle touch and stood by me through the making of this trove of tales.

The inspiration also came from while I was working with first learners from less privileged backgrounds, with whom verse, drama, charades, role play and spur-of-the-moment flashes of inspiration had enlivened our experience and made it truly enjoyable.